PUFFIN BOOKS

TUCHUS & TOPPS INVESTIGATE

THE UNDERPANTS OF CHAOS

Other titles by

SAM COPELAND

CHARLIE CHANGES INTO A CHICKEN

CHARLIE TURNS INTO A T-REX

CHARLIE MORPHS INTO A MAMMOTH

UMA AND THE ANSWER
TO ABSOLUTELY EVERYTHING

GRETA AND THE GHOST HUNTERS

Other titles by

JENNY PEARSON

THE SUPER MIRACULOUS JOURNEY
OF FREDDIE YATES

THE INCREDIBLE RECORD SMASHERS

GRANDPA FRANK'S GREAT BIG BUCKET LIST

TUCHUS & TOPPS INVESTIGATE

THE UNDERPANTS OF CHAOS

SAM COPELAND JENNY PEARSON

Illustrated by ROBIN BOYDEN *and* KATIE KEAR

PUFFIN

PUFFIN BOOKS

UK | USA | Canada | Ireland | Australia
India | New Zealand | South Africa

Puffin Books is part of the Penguin Random House group of companies
whose addresses can be found at global.penguinrandomhouse.com.

www.penguin.co.uk
www.puffin.co.uk
www.ladybird.co.uk

First published 2022
001

Text design by Janene Spencer
Printed and bound in Great Britain by Clays Ltd, Elcograf S.p.A.

A CIP catalogue record for this book is available from the British Library

The authorized representative in the EEA is Penguin Random House Ireland,
Morrison Chambers, 32 Nassau Street, Dublin D02 YH68

ISBN: 978-0-241-52106-9

All correspondence to:
Puffin Books, Penguin Random House Children's
One Embassy Gardens, 8 Viaduct Gardens, London SW11 77BW

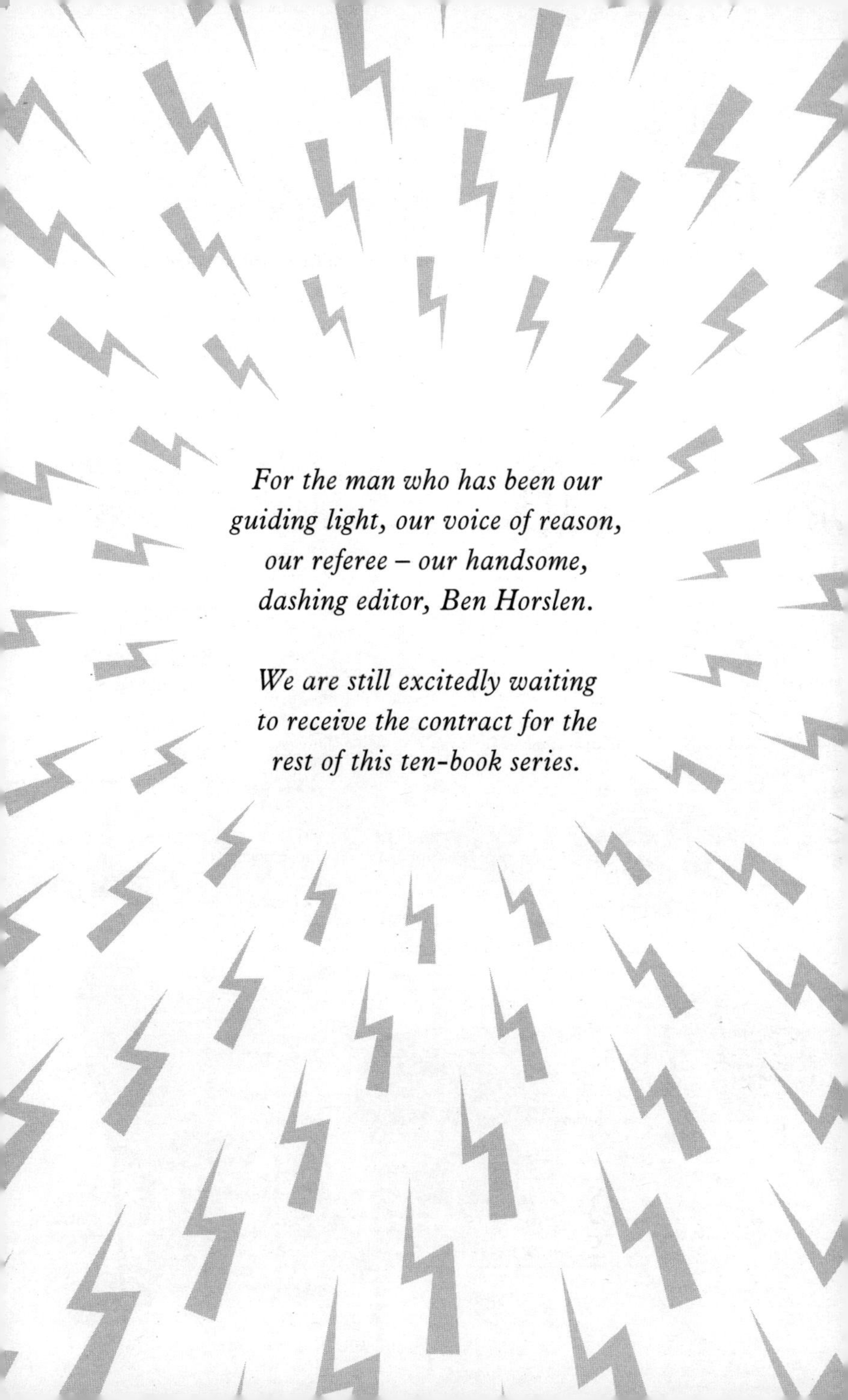

For the man who has been our guiding light, our voice of reason, our referee – our handsome, dashing editor, Ben Horslen.

We are still excitedly waiting to receive the contract for the rest of this ten-book series.

CHAPTER 1

AGATHA

My name is Agatha Topps, I'm nine years old and – prepare to be impressed – I'm a detective AND a spy!

Yup, a detective-spy, or a spy-detective if you prefer.

If you think that nine is too young to be a detective AND a spy, I'm here to tell you that you're wrong. Big time. Last year, I had a one hundred per cent success rate.

First, I solved the case of the Little Strangehaven School Scoffer. I told Mrs Applebottom that Ralph had eaten Thomas's Yorkie and, after she'd stopped freaking out and realized I meant a chocolate bar and not a small dog, Ralph had to miss out on his playtime.

I also solved the case of Mrs Applebottom's missing glasses (on her head), Dipa's missing pencil (behind her ear) and Sami's missing trainers (on his feet). What can I say? Clients aren't always the sharpest.

But this year my spy-detectivizing finally got properly tested because things got whole-other-level weird.

The first day I realized something was going on was the fourth day after I'd started in Year Four, the fourth day after Mum had had the twins, Nigel and Trevor, the fourth night I'd had pretty much no sleep, and the fourth morning I'd had to sort out my own breakfast as well as my other brothers' and sisters'.

I had been on duty with Bethany in the school chicken coop. It was our turn to give the hens their feed, but Margaret Hatcher and Mary Poopins had done a runner and it had taken a while to catch them, which meant I was a little flustered when I got back to class.

Our teacher, Miss Happ, was busy talking about how the money from our school fundraisers was going to be spent on a new automated library system. Everyone was a bit annoyed that the school council's request for a bouncy castle in the playground had been ignored and the money was going to some company called Minerva instead.

I was just settling into my seat when, all of a sudden, I felt a **SHIVER** ripple through the air.

I thought maybe I was imagining it. Maybe I was stressed because of the chickens, or maybe it was lack of sleep because my new baby brothers kept waking me up at night. Maybe it was just that everything was starting to get a little too much.

But no.

Every hair on my body felt like it was crackling with electricity.

'Did you feel that?' I said to Ernie, one of the boys on my table.

Ernie put down the Pritt Stick he was licking.

'Did I feel what?'

'That weird **SHIVER** in the air?'

Ernie shrugged and said, 'Nope,' then continued licking his glue.

The other boy on my table, Jordan Wiener (son of the school cleaner), stabbed his rubber with his pencil and said, 'You're what's weird, Agatha Topps.'

That was rude, but I ignored him because I understand that not everyone has the sort of highly tuned senses I have been blessed with.

While Miss Happ droned on about how much fun we were going to have studying the Romans this year, I scanned the room for the source of the strange **SHIVER**. Maybe a door or window was open and there was a draught?

It was an excellent thought, but a wrong one – there was nothing to explain where the **SHIVER** had come from.

I was still puzzling away when the music started. Music like I'd heard on that TV show where the contestants learn to dance and wear spangly costumes and a lot of orange make-up.

I scanned the room again, but I couldn't work out where the sound was coming from either. It almost felt like it was playing in my own head.

I stuck my finger into my left ear and waggled it about a bit to see if that would get rid of the music.

Nope. Still playing.

I found I couldn't stop myself from swaying along. In fact, I had an urge, a strong urge – an almost *overpowering* urge – to dance. This was VERY PECULIAR as I'm not much of a dancer.

My spy-detective senses were crackling. Something STRANGE was going down. I was a gazillion per cent sure about that.

I completed another scan of the room and noticed the whole class was swaying in time to the music. Even Ernie's tongue was lapping away in time to the beat.

I nudged him. 'What is that music?'

He didn't answer. Instead, he put his Pritt Stick down, pushed back his chair, strode over to Jordan and said, 'May I have this dance?'

I expected Jordan to bop him on the nose, but he didn't. He took hold of Ernie's hand, dipped a little curtsy and off they went, spinning round the classroom.

I could NOT believe my own eyeballs. I was mesmerized. I didn't want to stop watching, but, before I knew what I was doing, I had leaped to my feet and was striding over to Rahul, who was wiggling about in his chair.

No, Agatha, I screamed inside my head. *What are you doing?!*

Must dance!

DON'T DO IT!

Have to boxstep!

RESIST!!!

Left foot, right foot, slide and close!

RESISSSTTTT!!!!!

Then I heard my voice say, 'Hey, Rahul, fancy a foxtrot?'

I shook my head at him so he would know I didn't *really* want to.

He looked back at me with big, terrified eyes that said, *I want my mummy!*

But what he actually came out with was, 'I'd love to, Agatha. I thought you'd never ask.'

And then we were off, spinning and turning round the room.

Everybody was. Fifteen pairs of reluctant waltzers, plus Miss Happ, who had grabbed the teaching skeleton, Skeleton Bob, and was flinging him about wildly.

No matter how much I silently yelled at my hands to let go of Rahul, I couldn't stop. Something in me needed to dance.

I thought, *This is it. The end. I'll dance myself to death doing the promenade pivot step with Rahul. Hang on – how do I even know what the promenade pivot step is?!*

Then, just as suddenly as the first **SHIVER** had come, a second one rippled through the room.

Immediately, everyone stopped in their tracks and looked at their partner with utter disbelief.

Ernie tried to remove his hand from Jordan's. I think it must have been a little sticky from the glue because it took him a couple of tries to pull free.

Miss Happ threw poor Skeleton Bob callously to one side and looked round the class, her expression changing from confused to a bit annoyed.

'Everyone, sit down now, now!' she barked and everyone sat down on the floor. 'Not on the carpet!

In your seats!'

So we all got up again and sat down in our seats.

I have to admit, I was baffled. I leaned across the table to Ernie and Jordan and said, 'What was *that* all about?'

They looked at me with puzzled expressions.

'What do you mean?' Ernie said.

'What do *you* mean, "*What do you mean?*"? The dancing obviously!'

'What dancing?' Ernie said.

'Everyone was just dancing! You and Jordan were partners.'

'Shut your face!' Jordan hissed at me. 'We weren't dancing!'

'You were! You were quite good actually.'

'We were?!' Ernie sounded a little pleased.

'Shut up, Ernie!' Jordan hissed again. 'There wasn't any dancing! What are you talking about?'

'Didn't you feel the **SHIVER**?'

They looked at me blankly.

'Then we all got up and danced? Then the **SHIVER** came again?'

'Why are you saying shiver in that spooky voice?' Ernie asked, scraping glue out of his teeth.

Jordan scrunched up his already scrunchy-looking face. 'Yeah, you're the weirdest, Agatha. What are you even talking about?'

I looked round the classroom. Everyone was acting completely normally! Rahul was doodling in his exercise book; Bethany was twirling her hair and staring out of the window; Ralph was picking his nose. Nobody looked at all like they had any memory of our ballroom boogie!

And that's when I realized: I was the only person who could remember the Strangeness that had happened.

That is, until the new kid turned up.

LENNY
TUCHUS

LENNY
TUCHUS

CHAPTER 2
LENNY

I should have realized that there was going to be something seriously weird about a town called Little *Strange*haven. But, maybe if I had done, I would have refused to move there, and then I would never have met Agatha Topps.

Or become a spy-detective hero!

Little Strangehaven was my fifth school in four years. I've always moved around a lot because of Dad's job, but after he and Mum got divorced she promised we'd stay in Little Strangehaven permanently.

I live with my mum because Dad's job is super important. He's very cagey whenever I ask him *exactly* what he does, but I've figured it out. My dad is a spy for MI5. Why else would he suddenly have to cancel his visits and disappear without a trace for months at a time?

When Dad has time off from spying, he books into a hotel nearby and I get to stay with him there, which is quite fun. He always lets me order room service and I've got a whole collection of tiny shampoos and soaps as mementos.

I've also got a collection of Pez sweet dispensers that Mum buys to cheer me up when Dad cancels on me. At the last count, both collections are about equal.

Mum had told me that Little Strangehaven Primary would be no different to any other school I'd been to.

But then I saw it.

A huge, towering building, all pointy spires, gigantic doorways and gruesome-looking gargoyles staring down from the roof. Not particularly welcoming – more looming. And schools should not loom.

I knew immediately it was odd in some way. Although I didn't realize just *how* odd the place would turn out to be.

My last school, Cuckoo Lane Primary, was a modern building that had an arch over the gates with a cheery-looking rainbow painted on it. Although I hadn't stayed there long enough to make any proper friends, I suddenly really missed it.

I really missed a lot of things.

When I say 'things', I mainly mean Dad.

Mum parked up at the bottom of the school drive. I unfastened my seat belt, then paused before I climbed out.

'Why did Dad say he couldn't drop me off today?'

'Important work, love,' Mum said.

I nodded. He was probably defusing a nuclear bomb as we spoke.

'He said he'd try and pop round tonight if he can.'

'Brilliant!'

'But, Lenny, if he doesn't –'

'Don't worry, Mum. I understand.'

I said goodbye and, after Mum had pebble-dashed my face with lipsticky kisses and told me to 'Go get 'em, tiger!', I got my stuff out of the boot.

I took a deep breath and started up the long, sweeping drive. 'Have a wonderful day, my angel!' shouted Mum. 'Fly high and don't be afraid to tell the teacher if the work is too easy for you!'

Looking up at the school building, I half expected lightning to fork through the sky, thunder to crash overhead and bats to fly out of the towers. But they didn't. Not that day anyway.

I felt a horrible jittery-panicking feeling bubble up through me. If starting another new school wasn't bad enough, the school term had begun a whole week earlier. Everyone would already have made their friends.

'*Stop it!*' I said, but only in my head. I was being silly.

So, despite what turned out to be my extremely

well-founded concerns about Little Strangehaven, I thought about what my mum tells me to do when my insides feel all chaotic. That it's best to give a little whistle and get on with things.

Why she'd tell me to do that, knowing full well I can't whistle yet, I do not know.

'I'm sure this is a very friendly place,' I said out loud, then looked up at the very terrible and unfriendly-looking gargoyle that was sitting above the front doors.

I know it was made of stone, but something about its squinty eyes, massive nose and gnarled talons did not make me feel *that* reassured. But I reminded myself that I was used to being the new kid. I knew how to fit in, how to look cool.

So, collar up, baseball cap on my head at just the right angle, and carrying my favourite trombone and brand-new fencing kit, I said, 'Yo, gargoyle, you can't put Lenny Tuchus off with that horrible face of yours,' and pushed through the set of huge mahogany doors and strutted into the entrance hall of my newest brand-new school.

I peered down the nearest corridor and tried not to gulp – it looked dark and endless. Usually, it was bigger kids I had to worry about – leaping out from behind lockers and scaring me. Something told me that at Little Strangehaven Primary I should be ready for much worse.

I was just considering turning round and running for home when a very tall man with a very shiny bald head and extremely enormous nostrils appeared behind the reception desk.

I'd never seen nostrils like it. They were quite mesmerizing, like two black holes. I could almost feel their gravitational pull dragging me in. It was quite hypnotic.

'You must be Lenny Tuchus.'

I'd never heard my name said in such a terrifying way.

I gulped, then glared at him suspiciously. 'How do you know my name?'

'Because you have a big note on your chest

saying, "My name is Lenny Tuchus and I am new. Please help me.'"

I tore off the note, which my mum must have pinned to me at breakfast while I wasn't paying attention.

Right at that moment, a small, round man beetled up to the desk. He was wearing half-moon glasses, bright yellow trousers with small Scottie dogs embroidered on

them, and red braces that looked like they might snap any second under the strain of his tummy.

'Dr Errno,' he said, mopping his brow with a handkerchief, 'we really must discuss your proposal for this new library system!'

He didn't seem very happy.

Dr Errno's nostrils flared even wider and I wondered if he was going to suck the man in the bizarre trousers up into them.

'The thought of an *automated librarian* choosing books for pupils from an algorithm is simply too much to bear!' continued the little man. 'There's more to being a librarian than simply selecting books!'

'Really?' I said. 'Like what?'

'Like . . . Well, granted, that is a significant part of the job, but –'

Dr Errno cut him off. I wasn't really that interested anyway. 'Henry, this matter is closed. The Minerva sales director is coming today,' he said and nodded in my direction. 'Now see to this child.'

Then he swept off down the corridor, his black gown flapping behind him.

Funny-trouser-guy didn't say anything for a moment and I stood there, wondering what to do. If I could whistle, I would have done, to fill the awkward silence. But then he seemed to pull himself together.

'Where do you need delivering, young man and what's your name?'

'I'm Lenny Tuchus and I'm with Miss Happ, in Year Four.'

'Right, follow me, Tuchus. I'll show you to your classroom. I'm heading that way myself anyway. I'm off to the library. I'm the Custodian of Order.'

'You're a superhero?' I gasped.

'What? No. That's just what I call myself,' he said, peering at me. 'I'm the school librarian.'

I wasn't sure why a librarian would try to trick me into thinking he was a superhero. Probably to make himself sound more interesting.

'Well, I'm the school librarian – for the time being at least . . .' he went on. His voice seemed to get caught in his throat, but he did a big swallow, like a gulper fish, and continued. 'Onwards we go, young man.'

And he scuttled off down the corridor like a busy little beetle. I bolted after him.

A moment later, he suddenly stopped. 'Goodness gracious me, where are my manners? I was in a state of high emotion earlier and I completely forgot to introduce myself.' He grasped my hand and started shaking it vigorously. 'Pardon!'

'That's OK.'

'No! Pardon. Mr Pardon.'

Mr Pardon gave me a wink, his little raisin-like eyes sparkling behind his glasses, and suddenly Little Strangehaven didn't seem quite so scary.

'Now it's always difficult starting a new school. So, if you're ever feeling lonely, come to the library. I'm not one to boast, but it has won the Most

Orderly and Organized School Library Initiative award three years running! Not that that means much to *some* people.'

The MOOSLI award didn't mean much to me either. I didn't say that the library didn't *sound* like the most appealing place because that would have been rude, but I did think it.

'That's rather rude,' Mr Pardon said.

Ah – turns out I *had* said it. Sometimes I get a little confused and my mouth works without me realizing.

'I think you'll find that the library – this library in particular – *is* an exciting place.' He glared at me, but then a smile wiped his frown away. 'And remember – you're never alone with a book!'

I followed Mr Pardon down the corridor, my black trainers squeaking on the polished wooden floorboards.

'It's a very nice school,' Mr Pardon continued. 'The children are all very . . . pleasant.'

At that precise moment, a kid who looked like

a pencil (not literally, but he was very tall and skinny), with blond, spiky hair, charged by me and knocked my Spider-Man water bottle out of my hand.

'No running in the corridors, Master Wiener!' Mr Pardon shouted after him, but the kid didn't seem to hear.

'Who was that?' I asked.

'Jordan Wiener, son of the school cleaner,' Mr Pardon said and tutted. 'I've been here for thirty years and I can tell you with absolute confidence that this is the most normal and ordered school there is . . . for now.'

'The . . . most normal?'

'Oh yes. Totally and completely normal.'

I don't think Mr Pardon has been to as many schools as I have because Little Strangehaven certainly did not look that normal to me.

We stopped outside a heavy-looking door and Mr Pardon nodded for me to go in.

'You have a lovely day. And remember what I

said – do pop down to the library. Power lies in books, young man. Power lies in books.'

It was like the worst superhero slogan ever. *Power lies in books*. I mean, yeah, right! Ever seen Spider-Man battering his enemies to death with a copy of *The Hobbit*? But I nodded and said I would definitely come to the library soon. Which wasn't the complete truth because it was a lie.

Mr Pardon shuffled off round the corner. I took a deep breath, dialled up my coolness and pushed open the door to my new classroom.

I nodded at my new teacher, Miss Happ. She didn't nod back. Instead, she said, 'Class, this is our newest member, Leonard. Your table is over there.'

I was about to correct her – my full name's Lennox, not Leonard – but my tummy did this big dip when I saw where she was pointing. My seat was opposite that Jordan Wiener pencil-boy.

Worse luck.

But there were two other kids on my table: a

girl with scrappy blonde hair tied back in lopsided bunches, and a boy who was cleaning his glasses by licking them. Maybe one of *them* might make friends with me.

I weaved my way between the rickety desks, accidentally knocking someone with my trombone, and sat down next to the girl, who had a look on her face that said, '*Wow, who is this cool new guy in our class?*'

I gave her my best wink (which isn't easy because I can't close one eye without squinting with the other) and shot her with the finger-guns.

She stared like she'd never seen anyone like me before. Having been the new kid, like a gazillion times, I knew when I'd made an impression.

'Hey,' I said in my deepest voice. 'My name's not Leonard.'

She frowned. 'Really? What is it then?'

I decided I'd start off at this new school in the right way, and the right way is with a really cool nickname, so I said, 'You can call me Big Sick.'

bees
Agatha

CHAPTER 3
AGATHA

'Big Sick?' I repeated. 'Why do you want me to call you that?'

'It's my nickname,' Big Sick said.

'Why?' I said again. I couldn't understand why anyone would want to be called that.

'There's nothing big about him,' Jordan said. 'He's easily the smallest kid in the class, even smaller than Ernie and he's a year younger than everyone else.'

'He's right,' Ernie said. 'You're way smaller than me.'

'Maybe we should call him Little Puke,' Jordan suggested. 'That would suit him better.'

'I'd rather you didn't and I'm not *that* small.

I look taller in my other T-shirt,' Big Sick said, which I thought would be the stupidest thing I'd ever hear him say. However, I'd underestimated what else would come out of his mouth in the days and weeks that followed.

'I'm calling you Leonard,' I told him, for his own good really.

'OK,' he said.

Then, about two minutes later, he added, 'Or you could call me Lennox, which is my actual name. Or Lenny for short'

'Fine, but that doesn't mean we're friends. I am *extremely* picky when it comes to friends,' I said.

'Yeah, *that's* the reason no one hangs around with you,' Jordan said, and sniggered. 'Not because you're mega-weird and live in a dump.'

'I don't live in a dump,' I said, but I felt the hotness in my cheeks. My house isn't the tidiest, sure. We have a lot of clutter, but then we have a lot of people. I wouldn't say it was a dump, though.

'You're admitting you're weird then? Keep an eye out for her, Little Puke. She's a massive liar. No way would I do what she said I did.'

Lenny looked totally bamboozled, but before I could tell Jordan for the millionth time that everyone really *had* started ballroom dancing, Miss Happ barked at us to stop talking, settle down and do some work.

I sat, cleverly pretending to work, but actually silently plotting ways I could get back at Jordan.

The morning dragged on through a never-ending lesson about erosion and, just as I was about to fall asleep, I felt a **SHIVER** pulse through the room.

It made me gasp out loud.

'Oh, what now? You feel something again?' Jordan said *very* sarcastically. 'Was it a "shiver"?'

'It was, actually,' I said.

And then Lenny said, 'Yeah, I felt it too. What *was* that?'

CHAPTER 4
LENNY

Agatha didn't answer my question. Instead, her head started swivelling around frantically as if she was looking for something.

'Everything all right?' I asked politely.

She shushed me, very not politely, and said, 'Wait for it . . . wait for it . . .'

I looked about too, wondering what I should be waiting for.

Jordan Wiener rolled his eyes. 'Here we go. Is this where we all start doing the quickstep?'

Agatha ignored him, but Ernie began inspecting his arms and legs.

'I don't think they look like they want to start dancing,' he decided.

I have to admit, I had started to think that maybe Jordan was right and Agatha *was* the weird one.

But then a chicken marched in through the classroom door.

'Er,' I said, 'is that a chicken or am I seeing things?'

Agatha jumped to her feet. 'No! That's Mary Poopins. And I believe *that* is Margaret Hatcher right behind her. I must have left the cage open after I fed them this morning. Or . . . maybe this is the start of the Strangeness again!'

Before I could say, 'What did you call those chickens?', Mary Poopins turned round, raised her tail in the air and shot an egg out of her undercarriage.

And, when I say undercarriage, I mean bum. Because that's where eggs come from. I think. The egg flew across the room like a high-speed missile and **SMASHED** into the **WORK WE ARE PROUD OF** board.

'*Gahboowhah?!*' I said, because I do not know the correct response to seeing what could only be described as a military-grade chicken.

'Miss Happ, there's a chicken in the classroom and it shot an egg at us!' Ernie said.

Miss Happ didn't turn round from the whiteboard.

'Ernie, write down the date and title as you've been instructed and stop messing around.'

'But, miss, I'm allergic to feathers!' Ernie shouted, then sneezed and pulled his asthma pump out of his pocket and gave himself a couple of good blasts.

Mary Poopins strutted into the middle of the room, gave a loud cluck, her beady eyes watering, then bent over and stuck her bum in the air again.

The high-velocity egg-bullet flew across the

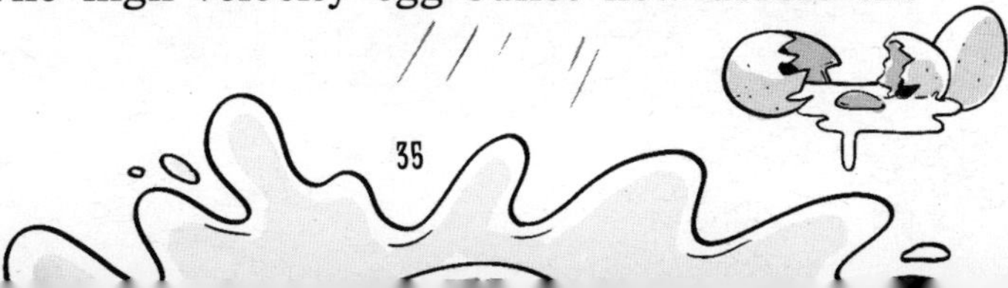

room and walloped Miss Happ on the back of the head.

That made her turn round.

'Somebody explain to me what's going on!' she boomed, wiping yolk and shell from her hair and flicking it on to the floor.

The whole class pointed at Mary Poopins, who looked like she was lining up another shot.

Miss Happ tilted her head, and said, 'Is that a chicken? In my classroom?'

Before anyone could answer, Margaret Hatcher pulled up alongside Mary Poopins and presented her bum to the world. I watched in horror as she proceeded to pebble-dash the classroom with eggs from her nether regions, like a feathery machine gun.

It was carnage. Eggs were splattering everywhere! Across the walls, on the floor – some poor kids even took shots to the body.

Everyone was screaming. Ernie was sucking frantically on his asthma pump. Jordan just stood there, sobbing really loudly, while egg dribbled down his face.

Agatha started tipping over desks to hide behind as more chicken reinforcements stomped into the classroom.

'Miss Happ! Everybody! Take cover! Albert Eggstein, Attila the Hen, Hennifer Lopez, Bird Lancaster . . . they're all here!'

Miss Happ grabbed her counting stick and started waving it about wildly. 'Get out! Get out *immediately*!'

But as military chickens don't speak humanish, and this lot seemed hell-bent on war, they just ignored her.

I had no idea how it was all going to play out. The chickens didn't look like they were going anywhere soon. They were firing round after round of eggs at us.

But that weird **SHIVER** pulsed through the room again. I looked at Agatha and could tell by her wide eyes that she had felt it too.

And then the second strange thing happened.

The chickens lowered their backsides and strutted out of the classroom, and everyone just stopped what they were doing.

Children stopped screaming, Jordan stopped sobbing, Ernie stopped pumping, and Miss Happ stopped waving her stick about.

For a moment, we all looked at one another, completely and utterly confused.

Then Miss Happ clapped her hands and said, 'Everyone back in your seats!'

Slightly dazed, we all did as we were told.

'Now who can explain to me why there are broken eggs all over the floor?' Miss Happ continued.

I raised my hand. 'It was the warrior chickens, miss.'

Miss Happ looked at me as if I'd just said the most peculiar thing in the world. Which I suppose is understandable.

'Warrior . . . chickens?'

'Yes! They were right here, spraying their egg-bullets all over the place! A whole herd of them – Margaret Hatcher and Mary Poopins and loads more. They just stomped in through the door and started a battle! It was mayhem!'

The rest of the class began to laugh. Well, everyone except Agatha, who was sitting very quietly, but staring at me very intently.

I couldn't understand why the others were pretending it hadn't just happened.

'Oh, come on! You were all here! What's going on?'

'It was them, Miss Happ – the new kid and Agatha – they were the ones throwing eggs!' Jordan Wiener shouted.

'It wasn't!' I shouted back. 'It was a pack of highly trained military chickens!'

'Enough!' Miss Happ slammed her hands on the desk. 'You and Agatha Topps have just earned yourselves some time in detention.'

I opened my mouth to try and explain, but

Agatha gave me a nudge with her pointy elbow.

Miss Happ turned back to the whiteboard, muttering about insolence, whatever that was, and Agatha whispered to me, 'You and I need to talk.'

'I know what I saw,' I said. 'Chickens. Chickens' bums. Eggs. Shouting . . . screaming . . . yolk everywhere . . .'

I trailed off. To be honest, I think I was in a state of severe shell shock. Ooh, I understand what that phrase means now!

But anyway I was just beginning to wonder if I *had* been seeing things when Agatha said, 'I remember those warrior chickens too.'

CHAPTER 5

AGATHA

I didn't mind being sent to the library for detention for three reasons:

1. Even though it was only the second week of term into Year Four, I'd spent pretty much every playtime hanging out there anyway, either reading books about spying and detectives or helping Mr Pardon keep 'everything right and orderly'. I like doing that because it makes me feel a bit calmer too. Let's just say nothing at my house feels very right and orderly.

2. I quite like the library. It feels a bit, I

dunno, *mysterious.* And I guess, as a top spy-detective, I'm naturally drawn to it. It was supposed to have been built hundreds of years ago. Some kids believe there's a secret room in the library where extra-special books are kept, but I've never found it.

3. It would give me a chance to interrogate Lenny about the whole **SHIVERY** chicken thing.

When I pushed open the big library door, Mr Pardon looked up from behind his desk, his half-moon spectacles balanced on his nose, and said, 'Ah, I believe this visit is for you both to reflect upon your behaviour in Miss Happ's class?'

He slid a very old and very big book into his desk drawer, whispering something to it, which was a bit weird, but, you know, librarians do love books.

'This is most disappointing,' he continued. 'Agatha, I didn't have you down as a troublemaker. And Tuchus, causing a scene on your first day. Worst of all, Miss Happ also informs me that you do not know the collective noun for chickens.'

Mr Pardon shook his head sadly.

I knew we were one hundred per cent innocent of the crimes of which we'd been accused, but there was something about the way Mr Pardon spoke, with such disappointment in his voice, that I heard myself mumbling, 'I'm sorry, Mr Pardon. Although not about the collective noun thing – that was all Lenny.'

I wasn't really sorry, though.

But I *was* determined to find out EXACTLY what was going on at Little Strangehaven, and this new kid was my very first clue – which was odd, considering he looked so clueless himself.

'I've set you the task of checking the order of the A section, Topps, and you the B, Tuchus,' Mr Pardon said. 'It's important that every book is in its proper place.'

'Didn't we already do that?' I said, because I'd helped Mr Pardon sort out those sections only the day before.

'One can never be too thorough, Agatha. You would not believe the ordeal I've been through this morning.'

Mr Pardon steadied himself on the desk. He looked visibly shaken.

'Did you see the herd of deadly egg-bombing chickens too?' Lenny asked.

'Flock!' Mr Pardon winced. 'Not herd!'

'Did you see the *flock* of deadly egg-bombing chickens too?' Lenny asked.

Mr Pardon gave him a long, hard stare, his usual sparkling eyes hardening for a moment. 'It's that sort of tall talk which got you into detention in the first place, Master Tuchus.'

Lenny did a little gulp.

'Sorry, Mr Pardon, but what ordeal did you go through?' I said. You never know, it could have been more Strangeness to investigate.

It wasn't.

Mr Pardon placed his hand on his chest and closed his eyes. 'It was Anita Parpalot!'

'Excuse me?' I said.

'The complete works of Anita Parpalot were on the incorrect shelf. I couldn't believe it!'

Lenny let out a little giggle, and his hand shot to his mouth.

'Do you find a misplaced Parpalot amusing, young man?'

Mr Pardon glared at Lenny, who stifled another giggle.

'It's no laughing matter,' Mr Pardon said. 'The woman from that dreadful company, Minerva, was here, doing her initial assessment. And there it was: Parpalot in among the Ms!'

'It doesn't seem *that* bad, Mr Pardon,' I said.

'That's not the worst of it. The biology section was all in a muddle too. *The Power of Antibiotics* by Penny Silling and *Bad Bacteria* by Mike Robes

had their spines facing inwards! Oh, the shame!'

'Still, on the scale of ordeals, I think kamikaze chickens win,' Lenny said.

Mr Pardon narrowed his eyes. 'Without order, there is chaos and *I* maintain order in this library, not some fancy computer! Now off you go – there's organizing to be done.'

While Lenny and I started checking through the A and B sections, Mr Pardon took the massive book out of his desk again and disappeared to the back of the library.

This was very handy as it meant Lenny and I could talk.

'It seems,' I said, 'that you and I were the only ones who could feel that weird **SHIVER** and remember what happened with the chickens.'

'Why are you saying shiver like that?'

'Like what?'

'You're saying it all spookily.'

'I'm *not*!'

'Yes, you are. You're all, "*shiiiiverrrr!*"'

I glared at Lenny and he stopped talking. Until he started again.

'Anyway,' he continued, 'I don't understand what's wrong with everyone! How could they forget *that*?'

'I don't know, but I'm going to find out. You see, Lenny,' I said, lowering my voice, 'I'm a spy-detective!'

He frowned thoughtfully, clearly impressed.

'What's a spider-tective? Do you investigate spider crimes?'

'Not a spider-tective! A spy-detective!'

Lenny looked at me blankly. 'You're saying the same thing.'

'A SPY-DETECTIVE!' I shouted. 'As in detective-spy!'

'OHHHHHH, cool! My dad's a spy!' Lenny said.

I found that *very* hard to believe.

'That's why he's away so much. He's always cancelling stuff with me because he has something super important to do. And while he can't ever say what – because of, you know, the Official Secrets Act – he's probably saved the world like a hundred times.'

I found that even harder to believe.

'Well, I am *actually* a detective *and* a spy,' I told him. 'And I'm going to discover what's causing the Strangeness at Little Strangehaven Primary.'

'How are you going to do that?'

'I have extensive spy and detective training,'

I told him.

'Prove it,' he said.

'What do you mean, *prove it*?'

'Do something spy-ish.'

'Like what?'

'I dunno – ooh, I *do* know! How about a commando roll?'

'Spies don't commando roll. They do stuff like interrogate people. And I need to interrogate you.'

'I'm not being interrogated by an amateur! What if it goes wrong and I end up losing a limb?'

'Lenny, do you know what interrogate means?'

'I do . . . not,' he admitted. Eventually.

'I just want to ask you some questions, that's all.'

'Hmmmm, I dunno. Do the roll and we can talk.'

'Lenny, I'm not doing a commando roll for you.'

'Knew you weren't actually a spy-detective,' Lenny said with a sigh. 'I reckon my dad does commando rolls all the time.'

'Oh, for goodness' sake, fine, if that's what it

takes!' I said and threw myself at the floor.

Now I haven't actually done a commando roll before, but I think it went quite well because Lenny said, 'Wow! You really *are* a spy-detective!'

And I said, 'Yes, I am.' And then surprised myself by saying, 'Want to team up?'

'You bet I do!'

I hadn't meant to offer Lenny employment. I only wanted to interrogate him – I really prefer to work alone – but the words just sort of tumbled out of my mouth. I think I must have been dizzy from my excellent rolling.

No matter. I was sure I could come up with some kind of assistant job for him. Maybe he could carry my night-vision goggles for me or something.

I held my hand out for a shake, but Lenny fist-bumped it instead, which was totally awkward.

'Right, first question,' I said, but then Mr Pardon poked his head round the bookshelf.

'I trust you are both doing what you're supposed to be doing?'

I quickly stuck a book on the digestive system by Ivana Pump back on to the correct shelf and smiled. 'Absolutely.'

Dratballs! I'd have to interrogate Lenny later, when no one else was around.

I decided to pay him a visit that very same evening . . .

CHAPTER 6

LENNY

I burst through the front door and shouted, 'I'm back!'

Mum bounded down the stairs. 'You're home! How was it?'

'Is Dad here? Is he coming?'

Mum shook her head and stroked my cheek. 'Sorry, love. He couldn't make it.'

I took a deep breath. You have to be brave when you're the son of an international spy. 'It's OK.'

'Come into the kitchen. I'll fix you a snack.'

I was kind of hungry, but I said, 'I might just go to my room for a bit.'

Later that evening, Mum asked me again how my first day of school had gone. I decided it was probably best not to mention the chicken attack, or the fact that I'd had a detention, even though it was all I could think about. She'd only overreact.

But, when she said, 'Did you make any new friends?' and looked at me with very anxious eyes, I said, 'Well . . . there's this girl called Agatha.'

I knew this would make her happy, even if Agatha wasn't exactly what I would call a friend. She was probably going to be more of an assistant because I'd decided *I* would be the person to discover what was happening at Little Strangehaven Primary.

'That's great, Lenny!' Mum put my chicken-and-matzo-ball soup in front of me and sat down at the table. 'You know, darling, I have a good feeling about this school. I'm thinking of joining the Parents' Association. Did you know they offer a tiddlywinks club, but no chess? That needs sorting. You could be a grandmaster, but you won't get there without the opportunity to play.'

I definitely liked the sound of being a grandmaster.

'And this Agatha sounds wonderful!'

'Wonderful' wouldn't be my first choice of word. I shovelled some soup into my mouth and thought about Agatha. Sure, she was a bit snarky, and she was *rubbish* at commando rolls, but apart from that she seemed all right.

'She's OK, Mum. Don't do that thing where you get all overexcited, though.'

'I never get overexcited,' she said and then grabbed my cheeks and planted a great big kiss on each of them, which I promptly wiped off with my sleeve.

'I'm just SO pleased you have a friend. You deserve a friend, Lenny. You're a great kid. The best kid. My favourite kid.'

She says that a lot. Dad does too, when I see him.

'I'm your only kid, Mum,' I reminded her.

'I'm just saying this Agatha obviously has excellent taste and I'm pleased you're settling in so quickly.' And then she walked off into the hallway, singing and doing a little dance.

I was pleased Mum was happy, and I suppose I was the teeniest bit happy too. It was nice to have someone who wanted to talk to me. Even if, when I say 'talk to me', I really mean 'interrogate me'.

I hadn't expected the interrogation to happen that very night, though.

I had just got into my Spider-Man pyjamas and crawled under the duvet when suddenly, and without warning, a foot swung in through my bedroom window.

I gave a little shriek and it was lucky I'd already had my bedtime wee or I might have done a tiny terror-piddle in my clean sheets. Not that that's ever happened before, OK?

The owner of the foot said, 'Shh, it's me, Agatha! Give me a hand.'

'Agatha?' I jumped out of bed and darted over to the window. She was clinging to the drainpipe – she must have climbed up on to the conservatory roof. I have to admit she looked very spy-like in her black tracksuit and balaclava. 'What are you doing?'

'I've come to ask you some questions. Now help me up!'

'How do you know where I live?'

'I'm a spy-detective, Lenny. It's literally my job to know these things.'

'But how?'

'Do you think we could maybe discuss this when I'm not half hanging out of a window?'

I grabbed hold of her leg and pulled her in. She landed on my carpet with a thump.

Mum must have heard because she shouted from downstairs, 'Lenny-Loo-Loo, what are you doing?'

'Er, nothing.'

'It didn't sound like nothing, Lenny-Loo-Loo.'

'Mum! Stop calling me that!'

I could hear Agatha stifling a giggle, then I heard Mum's footsteps on the stairs.

I hissed at Agatha, 'Hide!' No way would my mum be happy about a spy-detective climbing in through the window.

Quick as a flash, Agatha commando-rolled across my carpet and hid under the bed.

'If I open this bedroom door and find you practising your WWE moves with your teddies when you should be going to sleep, there will be trouble, Lenny-Loo-Loo!'

I heard Agatha giggle again when Mum mentioned my teddy-wrestling, but she fell silent the second Mum flung the door open. I jumped into bed and arranged my face to look as angelic as possible.

It must have worked because Mum said, 'Half an hour of reading, then lights off.'

When I was sure she was back downstairs, I dragged Agatha out from under my bed.

'That was close,' she said, pulling off her balaclava. It must have been quite hot because her face was bright red and it looked like there was steam coming off her head.

'What are you doing here? Won't your parents be worried you're missing? Couldn't this wait until tomorrow?' I said.

Agatha stood up and paced round my room. 'I'm the one who'll be asking the questions, *Lenny-Loo-Loo*!'

'If you call me Lenny-Loo-Loo again, it'll be the end of your spy-detectorivizing days! But seriously – won't your parents be panicking?'

'I'll be home before they even notice I'm gone. They're far too busy.'

Agatha said that very matter-of-factly, but when I said, 'Don't be ridiculous. How could your parents not notice that?', she got a bit defensive and said, 'They're just very busy, all right?'

She clapped her hands before things became too awkward, and got all organizational again.

'We need to start this investigation now. Who knows what might happen? One minute it's foxtrotting with Rahul, the next warrior chickens. Tomorrow all our heads could inflate to the size of wildebeest and explode.'

'Who's Will? And why is he a beast?'

'I said "wildebeest".'

I shrugged, still not clear who Will was. Agatha gave me an unreadable look.

'I meant that our heads could inflate to the size of a very large animal.'

'Do you really think so?' I gasped. 'I've grown

quite attached to my head.'

'Who knows? But the sooner we get to the bottom of what is happening at Little Strangehaven Primary the better.'

'OK,' I said, because she obviously needed someone with my leadership skills. 'I'm in.'

CHAPTER 7

AGATHA

It was easy to work out where Lenny lived because, after our last lesson, I secretly followed him as he skipped his way home.

He didn't notice me, not just because he was very involved in singing 'Let's Go Fly a Kite' extremely loudly, but because I am excellent at trailing people. I've had a lot of practice.

When I was first learning, I used to trail our old next-door neighbour, Mrs Haggis. I knew exactly what she was doing and when, whether it was her pensioners' belly-dancing class or her over-sixties yodelling lessons.

So at home time, hiding behind the coat pegs, I watched Lenny closely, trying to determine if he could be trusted, and whether he really was as clueless as he looked. I was worried I might have been a teensy bit hasty in asking him to help.

I saw him hopping from foot to foot as he tried to open the door to the boys' toilets by pulling it instead of pushing, and my instincts told me he probably wasn't going to be the brains behind the operation.

Never mind, I decided. Even though I'd accidentally invited him to join my team, I should probably treat him more as a piece of evidence.

So, that evening, I climbed up on to the conservatory roof of his rather fancy-looking house with the intention of examining my evidence. Very thoroughly.

My initial spy-detectoring findings were that Lenny had done a lot of stuff. Unlike my bedroom, his walls were plastered with certificates. Things I could only dream of doing. There were certificates for participation in coding club, horse riding, go-karting, badminton, dog grooming, gerbil grooming, grandma grooming, sewing, reaping, synchronized swimming, the tuba and so much more. There was even a Best Participant in Participating certificate.

'Wow, you've been busy,' I said.

'Thank you. Mum says she's sure we'll find my *thing* any day now!'

'I'm sure you will. Now to business.' I paced around with my hands clasped behind my back. 'The fact that we're the only ones who felt the **SHIVER** *and* remember the chickens must mean there's something special about both of us.'

'Oooh, I know!' Lenny said.

I paused, surprised and a little intrigued. 'Go on. In what way are you special?'

'I think in the *clever way.* My last teacher said I was special after I told her that no one really knows how aeroplanes fly, or how zips work, or why unicorns – which are basically just donkeys with horns – aren't real, but giraffes – which are basically leopard-horses with massive long necks – *are.*'

It took me a moment to process this. 'I don't think she did mean it in the clever way, Lenny.' I sat down on his bed. 'Dratballs!'

'What's up?'

'To be honest, my hypothesis as to why only I could feel the **SHIVER** and remember the Strangeness was that it was due to my heightened sensitivity and intelligence. But now the fact that you can feel them too means . . .'

'Means what?'

I looked at Lenny, who had a giant stuffed toy dog in a headlock. 'That I probably need to explore other avenues.'

'Maybe we have more in common than our super-brains,' Lenny said. 'We could go through and see if there are any other special connections?'

'Actually, that's not a bad idea. Tell me all

the things about you that are exceptional.'

He beamed. 'Buckle up. This could take some time.'

I didn't think that was likely, but then I didn't realize what Lenny considered to be exceptional.

'I can wiggle my ears. Not many people can do that.'

'Can you really?' I have to admit I was a little impressed because in the past I'd tried and failed.

'Yeah, look!'

Lenny then started to waggle every part of his face other than his ears.

'I hate to break it to you, but you can't wiggle your ears.'

His face fell. 'I can't? I thought I could.'

'Don't worry, neither can I.'

'Well, that's it! We've found the connection. We can both feel the **SHIVER** and remember the Strangeness because neither of us can wiggle our ears! I really thought that was going to take a lot longer.'

At first, I thought he was joking, but he looked so pleased with himself, I realized he wasn't.

'Lenny, lots of people can't wiggle their ears. I don't think that's the connection.'

He looked a bit upset while he mulled that over, then a big smile spread across his face.

'It's OK. We just have to figure out what else I'm great at . . . Ooh, I know!'

I was almost too scared to ask. 'Go on . . .'

His chest puffed up as he said, 'I can breathe underwater.'

I glanced at the side of his neck to see if he had gills. He didn't. 'Lenny, you cannot breathe underwater. No human can.'

'This human can! All you need is a snorkel.'

'OK . . . That's *probably* not it either. What else have you got?'

'I can burp on demand?' he said, then did the hugest burp in my face.

Obviously, I had to do an even bigger burp in return.

'Wow! That was amazing, Agatha!'

'Thank you, but burping is also not the connection. I'm pretty sure Ernie and half the rest of our class can do that too.'

'I can also fart extremely loudly without warning. I stopped a bus once because the driver was so surprised.'

'I never fart,' I said, which wasn't strictly true, but Lenny didn't need to know that.

'Hmmm.' Lenny looked like he was thinking again, then suddenly whipped up his Spider-Man pyjama top. 'Maybe my special powers come from Bernard?'

'Bernard?'

'I have a mole that looks like a second belly button, see?'

'Yes, I see,' I said, pulling a face. 'But what's that got to do with a Bernard?'

'That's his name, of course! Bernard the Belly-Button Mole. Do you have a Bernard?'

'No, Lenny. As astonishing as this may sound,

I do not have a mole called Bernard who looks like a second belly button.'

He put his hand on my shoulder and said, 'I'm sorry,' as if not having a belly-button mole was a bad thing. Then he crumpled up his face and screwed his eyes shut.

'What are you doing now? You're not going to do one of those super-loud farts, are you?'

He opened one eye. 'I'm thinking as hard as I can.'

I waited for a few minutes, while he sat there looking like he was about to strain a muscle.

Eventually, I said, 'Lenny, maybe we need to stop for now. You look like you're in pain and we don't seem to be getting anywhere. I'm going to go home and think more about who or what could be behind all the Strangeness and those **SHIVERS**.'

Lenny relaxed his face and shrugged. 'OK, I'll keep thinking about all the things I'm excellent at and bring you a full list tomorrow.'

'Sounds wonderful,' I said, not completely truthfully, and climbed back out of the window.

Lenny came over and watched me as I shimmied down the drainpipe.

'Thanks for dropping by. That was actually kind of fun!'

'I'm only here in a professional capacity,' I told him.

'OK, bye! It was fun being professional with you!' he said and waved at me the whole time I was climbing down. I turned back when I was halfway along the street and could see him in his window, still waving.

I felt my lips spread into a smile. I didn't like to admit it – I'm not one for hanging around with other kids – but I'd had fun too. I had learned A LOT about Lenny very quickly and, despite the supersonic farting and his fondness for Bernard, he was actually kind of OK.

CHAPTER 8

LENNY

The next morning, I was in THE BEST mood for two reasons. Number one, my dad had called to say he was taking me out after school and, number two, spending the night thinking about all the things that are special about me made me feel very positive. It was also quite exciting to be leading a proper spy-detective investigation, just like my dad. Ooh, maybe I could ask him for some tips!

I skipped down the street to school, still feeling pretty wonderful. At least until I heard someone yell, 'HA! LOOK AT LITTLE PUKE SKIPPING!'

Jordan Wiener was standing by the great iron school gates. He was looking particularly pencilly and extra spiky. I stopped skipping, and walked past, ignoring him and trying not to blush.

'HA! LOOK AT LITTLE PUKE BLUSHING!' he shouted again.

I was really starting to dislike pencils by this point.

I have to admit that when Agatha came out of nowhere, and went striding up to Jordan, I was happy to see her. I was even happier when she whispered something in Jordan's ear and he turned white and ran away.

'What did you say to him?' I asked as we walked to class together, very pleased with my new sort-of friend, sort-of assistant.

'I said you were a massive telltale and would definitely report him to the head teacher.'

'WELL, WHY DID YOU SAY THAT?' I snapped, thinking I might have to reconsider the sort-of friend, sort-of assistant thing. 'Now everyone will think I'm a blabberer. I'll never make any friends!'

Agatha looked a bit put out, until I told her I'd come up with some more ideas about what we might have in common. I went through the list I had stored in my head as we made our way to the classroom.

'I once swallowed a bee. That might have given me my super-sensing powers. Have you ever swallowed a bee?'

'No, Lenny.'

'OK, strike that off the list. I also swallowed a tiny plastic dinosaur . . .'

'I have never swallowed a tiny plastic dinosaur.'

'How about a penny? Have you ever swallowed a penny?'

Agatha paused outside the classroom door and sighed. 'Is your whole list made up of things you've swallowed?'

'There is quite a large section on that,' I admitted.

'Lenny, you really shouldn't swallow stuff that isn't food.'

I was about to tell her I hadn't swallowed those things on purpose, and that we could move on to the list of objects I've had stuck up my nose, when a deep and terrifying voice boomed out behind us.

'Should you two not be in class by now?'

'Dr Errno!' Agatha said, visibly cowering before the head teacher. 'We were just heading in.'

'Lateness is not tolerated at Little Strangehaven Primary.' Dr Errno suddenly glared at me, his nostrils flaring even wider. 'Are you staring at me?'

'Nose, sir! I mean no, Dr Errnose, sir! No! I didn't mean nose! I meant no, sir, Dr Errno, sir.'

I winced.

'What's your name, boy?' Dr Errno asked, his eyes drilling into mine.

'Tuchus, sir! Lenny Tuchus.'

'Well, Mr Tuckus –'

'No, not "Tuckus". It's pronounced Tuccccchhh-uss,' I corrected, helpfully. Dr Errno glared at me even harder. He didn't look very grateful to be corrected. 'You have to really roll the middle of your word in your throat. Like this: Tuccchhh-uus. You try!'

'Took-hus . . .?' he said, uncertainly.

'That'll do,' I said.

He glared harder still. 'As I was saying, you had best watch yourself, Mr Took-hus. Because I'll be watching you. Now into class before I am forced to punish you.'

I'm not proud of it, but I gave a little whimper and started frantically tugging at the classroom door, desperate to get away from Dr Errno and his hypno-nostrils as fast as I could. But, for some reason, the door was locked. I pulled and pulled –

I think at one point I even had both feet on the door frame to give me more power – but it was no good. It just wouldn't open.

Eventually, I stopped yanking and panted, 'Please don't punish us, Dr Errno.'

Dr Errno looked me up and down and said, 'I have never before witnessed anything quite like that.'

Which I would have taken as a compliment if his face hadn't been quite so stony.

Agatha then very calmly pushed the door and it swung open.

'Come on, Lenny,' she said. 'I'll talk you through how doors work later.'

What a good assistant.

'I think it would be a *very* good idea for you to commence your lessons immediately, young man,'

Dr Errno said, looking at me with one dark, angular eyebrow raised. 'I imagine there is much that you do not know.'

Then he stalked off down the corridor, all menacing and villainy.

'He does *not* look like someone you want to get on the wrong side of,' I said.

'Definitely,' Agatha said as we sat down at our table with the others. 'Everyone's terrified of Dr Errno, even the teachers.'

'I'm going to stay well out of his way,' I told her.

'Could be difficult,' Agatha said.

'Why?'

'Because, of all the suspects who could be behind the Strangeness, Dr Errno is top of my list.'

CHAPTER 9

AGATHA

I had come to realize it was going to be difficult to work out why Lenny and I were the only ones who could feel the **SHIVER** and remember the Strangeness. I found it very hard to imagine us having *anything* in common.

So I decided to turn my attention to finding out the source of the Strangeness instead. Somebody – or *something* – had to be responsible for it. I just had no idea who or what.

My reasons for putting Dr Errno as number one on my list of suspects were twofold:

1. My excellent spy-detective instincts. There was something in my bones telling me that he

was the most likely culprit, mainly on account of him having a *bit of an evil feel* about him.

2. I didn't have any other suspects.

While this approach might not seem that scientific, I didn't think I should ignore a gut feeling – especially when we were talking about a gut as strong as mine.

After a really good lesson about Roman toilets, I told Lenny we would not be going outside at playtime, but to the library to discuss how we were going to investigate the Strangeness.

Mr Pardon wasn't there, which was unusual, but did mean that we wouldn't be interrupted.

I found us a spot among the towering bookshelves and we sat down on the faded carpet. Portraits of past head teachers loomed over us. I then told Lenny about my probably-most-definitely excellent plan.

'We are going to watch and wait.'

It was dazzling in its simplicity. Obviously, Lenny couldn't see that, though.

'Watch . . . and *wait*?' he said in a manner that was frankly rather rude, considering I was his boss. 'That's not a plan.'

I had to let out a really long breath and remind myself that not everyone is in possession of a phenomenal mind like mine.

'We wait,' I continued, 'until the next strange event happens, and then . . .' I paused to build the tension, so he could appreciate how truly extraordinary the plan was.

'And then?'

'We investigate!'

Lenny did not react like he was supposed to. He wrinkled up his nose and said, 'Sounds like we're doing nothing.'

'We're not doing *nothing*. We're *waiting*.'

'Waiting for what?'

I took another deep breath. 'For the Strangeness to happen. And when it does, Lenny-Loo-Loo, we'll be ready and waiting!'

'You'll be the opposite of ready and waiting if you call me Lenny-Loo-Loo again.'

'What? That doesn't even make sense.'

'Yeah, it does. You'll be . . . unready and

unwaiting because I'll have done something – I'm not quite sure what – but it will be so effective you can't be ready or waity any more.'

At this point, I thought it best to ignore everything he was saying. He was only my assistant after all.

'OK, *Lennox*. Next time we feel the **SHIVER**, we need to check on Dr Errno and see if he's anywhere nearby, looking suspicious. We have to find the evidence that will bring him to justice and put an end to the Strangeness once and for all!'

I have to say it was quite a good speech, only ruined when Lenny said, 'If it's him.'

'Of course it's him! He's an evil-looking head teacher! Have you ever even read any books? It's *always* the evil-looking head teacher.'

Annoyingly, Lenny still had an uncertain look on his face. Or maybe it was confusion. It was usually confusion with Lenny, so I gave him the benefit of the doubt.

'Look,' I continued slowly, 'everyone knows all

head teachers hate kids, and you have to admit Dr Errno has a strange feel about him . . . and, to be honest, it's the only lead we have to go on. For now.'

'And I suppose he *does* have those awfully hypnotic nostrils.' Lenny nodded. 'But I still don't understand why a head teacher would want to cause all this weird stuff to happen in his own school.'

'True. And that's something we need to find out.'

It was at this point that we heard the library door creak and then the sound of a key in the lock.

'What was that?' Lenny whispered. 'Have we just been locked in . . . the *library*? Ugh – worst day ever. What are we supposed to do in here for entertainment?'

'Shh, let me see what's going on.'

I scurried to the front of the library on my hands and knees, and then whispered back to tell Lenny what I could see.

'It's Mr Pardon,' I said. 'And he looks a teensy-weensy bit . . . stressed.'

CHAPTER 10
LENNY

I had to see for myself what a stressed librarian looked like, so I crawled along to the end of the row of bookshelves in a very spy-detectory-like manner.

Sure enough, there was Mr Pardon, sitting at his desk and rocking back and forth, clutching that giant book to his chest.

'Yes, bookums-snookums, I hear you. I will open you. Soon, I promise. Yes, this is *my* library! No, I won't let them take it from me!'

'Who the heck is he talking to?' I whispered, looking around.

'Himself?' Agatha said.

At that moment, somebody tried to open the

library door. When it didn't budge, they started knocking.

'Mr Pardon, we're here for the meeting with Minerva.'

It sounded like Dr Errno.

Mr Pardon's eyes bulged behind his glasses. I guessed he wasn't keen on this meeting. But he didn't have any choice because a key was put into the lock, the door swung open and Dr Errno marched in, leading a woman wearing an electric-blue suit and a big smile.

She was carrying a briefcase with a logo of an angry-looking owl with lasers for eyes. In a circle around the cyber-owl were the words MINERVA AUTOMATED LIBRARIAN SYSTEM. Dr Errno was laughing and chatting and being very un-Errno-like.

Mr Pardon leaped up from his seat and slipped that massive book of his back into a desk drawer.

'Ah, Mr Pardon, you *are* here. Wonderful!'

Dr Errno began. 'This is Ms Pamela Stranglebum. She's here to look over the library again ahead of the upgrade, as we discussed.'

I nudged Agatha and snorted – 'Stranglebum!'– but she shushed me.

Ms Stranglebum shook Mr Pardon's hand very ferociously.

'Goodness, it's even more outdated than I remember!' she said, with a tinkly laugh. 'You really are very right to call on my services, Dr Errno.'

'B-b-b-but . . . but this library is full of history and tradition . . .' Mr Pardon stuttered, getting very red-faced.

'While we must not forget the past, Mr Pardon,' Dr Errno said, clapping his hands together, 'we must also look to the future.'

'And I'm very much looking forward to dragging this relic into the twenty-first century,' Ms Stranglebum said, gazing round the room.

Mr Pardon didn't respond, but, from the look

on his face, I wouldn't have been surprised if steam had started shooting out of his ears.

'Dr Errno,' Ms Stranglebum said, placing her hand on his sleeve, 'there's much work to be done here, but I am confident that Minerva can transform this musty graveyard of paper into a multi-aspect reading hub of the future. The Minerva Automated Librarian System not only scans books; it also scans children's *brains*. Using

each child's intellectual data, we can then pinpoint reading material of an appropriate level to expand your pupils' knowledge in key curriculum areas in which they are identified as falling short.'

Dr Errno gazed adoringly at Ms Stranglebum and gave a long sigh. 'My goodness me. Incredible!'

Mr Pardon watched with a look of pure horror as Ms Stranglebum stalked round the library, pointing at things with a silver pen.

'The probes could go *there*, docking points *there*, and *that's* an excellent place for the recharging capsules. Oh, I cannot wait to get my hands on this place!'

'Perhaps we can discuss the final points of the contract over tea in my office?' suggested Dr Errno, with what seemed almost to be a blush, as he led Ms Stranglebum to the door. 'If you'll excuse us, Mr Pardon . . .'

Once they'd gone, Mr Pardon slumped into one of the beanbags in the quiet space and disappeared from view as it swallowed him up.

A very strange sound started rattling about the library.

I looked at Agatha. 'What is *that*?'

'That, Lenny, is Mr Pardon crying.'

'Are you sure? It sounds more like a rusty walrus being strangled!' I replied in my best spy-detective whisper.

Agatha put her finger to her lips and shook her head very loudly, which immediately got Mr

Pardon's attention. He flailed about in his beanbag, finally managing to wriggle to his feet.

'Who's there?' he demanded, his head swivelling about wildly.

Agatha walked out from behind the bookshelf, giving me a look.

'That was the worst spy-whisper I've ever heard,' she said, which seemed a bit unfair when it had clearly been her loud head-shaking that had given away our location. 'And how can a walrus even be rusty?' she added, which was a more reasonable question, I admit.

'Is everything OK, Mr Pardon? You seem like you're upset about something,' Agatha said. 'Lenny and I were just back here, doing some reading.'

Mr Pardon lifted his glasses and dabbed his eyes with his sleeve. 'Everything's fine, dear child. Thank you for asking.'

'Who was that woman?' I asked.

Mr Pardon sighed. 'She is the future, apparently. Dr Errno has decided he wants the "internet" in the library. And "AI-assisted, book-recommending robots".'

'But that's awf– actually, that sounds awesome!' I said. I mean, who wouldn't want ROBOTS in their school library?!

'Well, it's not awesome,' snapped Mr Pardon. 'Do you know how *unreliable* technology is? This could mean the end of librarians. The end of reading! The end of order!'

'We can't let that happen!' cried Agatha, who OF COURSE didn't want book-recommending robots because of her lack of imagination.

'No, we can't let that happen,' I said, perhaps not very convincingly as I was already kind of sold on the idea of a cyborg librarian who might come with a laser gun.

Mr Pardon shook his head sadly. 'Unfortunately, it's Dr Errno who has the power. The contract is agreed. My days are numbered.'

'But it's not fair, Mr Pardon. You've been at this school longer than anyone,' Agatha said.

'Do you think these robots will be extra strong? You know – able to crush a car?' I asked.

'Lenny!' Agatha snapped. 'Not the time.' She turned to Mr Pardon. 'I'm so sorry, sir.'

'It has been my life's work keeping order in this library, but it seems that's not enough for Dr Errno.' He forced a smile. 'But I suppose that's life. Now you two had better run along. You're already late for lessons.'

As we raced back through the corridors, Agatha said, 'We really have to find out what Dr Errno is up to now. Maybe if we can prove he's behind the Strangeness –'

'He'll get arrested by the school police and there'll be no robot librarians!'

'There's no such thing as school police. And you need to stop going on about robots. Let's just hope the Strangeness happens soon, so we can investigate properly,' Agatha said. 'In the meantime, Lenny, we wait.'

When I arived home after school, I looked up and down the road, but couldn't see Dad's car. I sat on the wall, hoping he'd turn up any minute.

Mum must have spotted me because she came outside, holding a Pez dispenser.

'Lennox, my love, he phoned. He can't make it today.'

I almost didn't want to take it from her, but it was the Donkey Kong one I'd been after for ages. I sighed. Sometimes the life of a spy isn't an easy one.

'He said he'll try to drop by tomorrow instead.'

Back in my room, I put Donkey Kong on the shelf with all the others and phoned Agatha.

I was beginning to have some serious concerns over her two-step waiting-and-investigating plan because we seemed to be permanently stuck in Step 1: waiting. And waiting is boring. And sometimes hard to do.

It was time to show her who was in charge.

'Agatha,' I said forcefully, 'I want to be more

than a spy-detective who waits for stuff to happen. I want to take control!'

And she said, 'OK, we'll discuss it tomorrow.'

I think she was bored of waiting too.

I had no idea how I was going to take control, but I was sure I'd think of something.

CHAPTER 11
AGATHA

The following day, over lunch in the dining hall, Lenny sucked up his custard through a straw, and told me about his plan to rugby-tackle Dr Errno to the floor and wrestle him until he confessed. Meanwhile, I did something far more useful and quietly contemplated the possible causes of the **SHIVER**.

Maybe it wasn't Dr Errno. It was possible I had that wrong. Unlikely but possible. Perhaps the Strangeness was the result of an invisible gas or freak radio waves.

But then, as I was shovelling a third helping of pudding into my mouth, we felt the **SHIVER** ripple through the dining hall.

I dropped my spoon and it clattered into my bowl.

'Did you feel that, Lenny?'

Lenny shot custard out of his nose in surprise. 'Matzo balls! It's happening.'

I was a whole jumble of feelings. A bit worried, of course. A bit relieved we didn't have to go through with Lenny's wrestling idea, but mainly excited that something was afoot.

'Stay alert, Lenny. What do you see? Anything out of the ordinary?'

Lenny looked round the room. 'Nothing yet.'

My stomach did a flip-flop. Waiting for something to happen was intense.

A few seconds passed, everyone happily chomping through their sponge and custard, oblivious to the chaos that was about to hit.

'Wait for it . . . wait for it . . .' I said, with absolutely zero clue as to what we were actually waiting for.

But then I started to feel a tingling sensation around my chin. I looked at Lenny and saw he was scratching his cheeks.

Interesting.

'Does your face feel weird?' I asked as my chin-tingling ramped up a level.

'Yeah, a bit hot and bubbly.'

'Mine too.'

The tingling turned to itching and then to a fizzly scratching sensation.

Then a fiery burning.

Suddenly a full-on massive bushy beard sprang out from Lenny's chin. It was horrific. It looked like he had a badger strapped to his face.

'Lenny, now don't panic, but you've just grown a badger – I mean a beard,' I said as calmly as I could because a good spy-detective never panics.

His hand shot to his face. ‘No!’ he wailed. ‘I don’t want a badger *or* a beard! Everyone will laugh at me if I have a beard and I’ve got nowhere to keep a badger . . .’

‘No one will laugh,’ I said. This was an accidental lie because people were already starting to point at Lenny and snigger.

‘I don’t know how to shave,’ moaned Lenny. ‘And my dad isn’t even around to teach me!’

‘Don’t worry!’ I said, trying to calm his panic. ‘You look . . . fine.’

‘Fine?!’

‘Distinguished even. I actually think it might be an improvement.’

‘No nine-year-old kid can carry off a beard successfully, Agatha!’ He looked at his reflection in the back of his spoon. ‘Gah! I look like Rabbi Shulman!’

‘I think you need to calm down. It’s only hair.’

‘That’s all right for you to say! You don’t have a massive furry blanket sprouting from your chin, do you? Do you?! DO YOU?!!!' Lenny said, shaking me by the shoulders.

But then he stopped, tilted his head and said, 'Oh, hang on, scrap that – you actually do.'

'I do?'

'Yup, a ginger beard that a grizzled old pirate would be proud of, Agatha. It appeared just now when I was shaking you. Oh – I hope I didn't shake it out of you.'

'I think it's down to the **SHIVER**, Lenny.'

I checked myself out in the back of my own spoon. I did indeed have a gingery beard. Surprising, considering I have whitish-blonde hair. But I have to say I didn't mind it – it made me look quite wise and dangerous.

The screams that were rising up around the dining hall suggested that not everyone was taking as kindly to their new facial fuzz as I was.

In fact, it was *mayhem*.

There were beards sprouting *everywhere*.

Wherever I looked, there were children

growing beards. Boys, girls, the teachers sitting at the staff table – Miss Happ included. She was crying and trying to pull hers off, but it was no use: it was well and truly attached.

In among the commotion, I tried to keep a cool head and do some top-class spy-detectoring. I scanned the room carefully, looking for clues, while my assistant seemed more interested in twirling the end of his beard with a fork.

Luckily, my spy-detectoring instincts were on fire and I noticed, out of the corner of my eye, that the double doors of the dining hall were swinging back and forth, as though someone had just left the scene of the crime!

I raced over, pulled them open and looked down the corridor just in time to see the flap of a head teacher's black gown turning the corner.

CHAPTER 12
LENNY

Once I was over the shock of suddenly becoming a beard-owner, it was actually quite interesting to see the different beards that people had grown.

Jordan Wiener, for example, only had a tiny sprouting of blond fluff growing on his top lip. However, Ernie's entire face was covered in hair, like some kind of child werewolf. I half expected him to leap on the table and start howling at the moon. One of the dinner servers had such a huge white beard that, even though I'm Jewish, it still made me want to sit on her knee and tell her what I wanted for Christmas.

I suppose I may have got a little distracted from the detectoring I was supposed to be doing, but, in

my defence, I'd never seen a room full of furry-faced children before. Instead of looking for clues, I found myself rating the beards out of ten.

I thought it was probably best not to admit to this, though, when Agatha stormed up to me, grabbed my elbow quite roughly and said, 'Did you see what I just saw?'

I had a fifty-fifty choice. Fess up to my assistant about losing focus, or pretend I knew what she was talking about. Like all great leaders, I was pretty sure I could wing it, but I decided not to lie this time.

'Er, no, I –'

'I thought so! Suspicious that he was here, right?'

'Yes, Agatha, very suspicious. Just to clarify – you're talking about Jord–'

'Dr Errno, of course! Like you just said.'

That worked out better for me than I'd expected.

'We need to follow him, quick. I saw him out in the corridor!'

But we couldn't be quick because, right then, another **SHIVER** thrummed through the air.

I clasped my hands to my face.

'My beard's gone,' I said. 'Yours too!'

'Shame.' Agatha stroked her bare chin thoughtfully. 'I wouldn't have minded keeping that.'

One by one, everyone in the dining hall stopped screaming, took their hands away from their faces and looked around, dazed and confused.

'They've all forgotten again,' Agatha said.

'Our super-brains haven't, though!'

'I don't think our brains are what is connecting us,' Agatha said.

'You thinking Bernard the Belly-Button Mole again?'

'You really need to let that one go, Lenny.'

While I tried to think what else our connection could be, Miss Happ shouted at everyone to either sit down and continue eating or take their dirty plates back to the hatch. With everyone busy, Agatha grabbed my elbow and we darted out into the corridor. She dragged me all the way to the end and then came to an abrupt stop.

'Dratballs! We need to find Dr Errno. Which way do you think he went?'

'Dunno. Left or right or maybe straight on?'

'Helpful as always. Let's head towards the staffroom,' Agatha said, dragging me by the elbow again (she does like an elbow drag).'We need to find out how he's doing it.'

'I have a new theory,' I said, because one had just popped into my head. 'He might be hypnotizing the school with his massive hypno-nostrils.'

Agatha didn't respond immediately. She was probably considering my suggestion very carefully.

In fact, I think she was still considering it when we turned the corner and spotted Dr Errno and that Stranglebum woman standing in reception.

We scurried down the corridor with our backs flat against the wall so we wouldn't be seen.

'I'll be back tomorrow, to start the installation process, Dr Errno,' Ms Stranglebum was saying.

'Looking forward to it,' Dr Errno said. He smiled and showed her all his teeth, and then guided her out.

'Hmmmm,' Agatha hmmmed at me. 'There's something about that Minerva woman that I don't like.'

'Do you think she has something to do with the **SHIVER**?'

'It's a bit suspicious she was just here when it happened. And there was none of this **SHIVERY** madness going on before Minerva appeared on the scene. It could be a coincidence, but as good spy-detectives we should be open to all possibilities.'

'I agree, including Bernard.'

Agatha closed her eyes and took a deep breath. The recent events must have been a lot for a spy-detective's assistant to process.

Eventually, she looked at me again and said, 'Can I come to your house tonight for a debrief?'

I would have liked a debrief (it sounding like something an assistant shouldn't be doing unsupervised), but I had other plans. 'Sorry, my dad is probably definitely coming to see me tonight.'

'Can't you cancel?'

'Um, no, I can't cancel. I haven't seen him in ages.'

'Why's that?'

'Because he's been *very* busy being a spy.'

'Right.'

I did not like the tone of that 'right'. But I think Agatha was probably worried about having a debrief without me.

'Look, maybe I can pick his spy-brains. I bet he has loads of ideas. He'll probably solve the case straight away!'

Agatha shrugged. 'Yeah, maybe. I guess I'll just catch up with you tomorrow then.'

'OK! See you tomorrow! Have a good evening!' I said, and raced off home, excited to see my dad.

CHAPTER 13
AGATHA

That evening, as I was doing the washing-up, I went over and over the events that had led up to the **SHIVER**. It couldn't have been a coincidence that Dr Errno and Ms Stranglebum were in the vicinity when everyone started sprouting beards. And, thinking about it, she'd also been in school with Dr Errno on the day of the ballroom dancing and chicken attack.

'How is this happening? *Why* is this happening?!' I said out loud, frustrated that we hadn't found any real clues and weren't really any closer to discovering what was going on.

I left the dishes to air-dry and stuck Nigel and Trevor's bottles in the sterilizer, then went upstairs and lay down on my bed. I screwed up my eyes really tight because it helps me block out all the noises from around my very noisy house. The neighbours sometimes complain, but, as my dad says, 'What do you expect from a house with eight kids and two dogs?' Still, I find if my eyes are closed I can concentrate better on thinking.

'You all right? You look like you need a poo.'

I opened my eyes. 'Lenny! What are you doing here?'

I felt a wave of embarrassment billow through me. Lenny was at my house. People weren't supposed to see my house.

'I hope you don't mind me dropping round. Turns out I'm free after all. I tried to phone –'

'We've been cut off!' I said quickly, so as not to make a big deal about it.

'A guy with a tattoo of a squirrel on his arm let me in.'

'That's my dad.'

'Your dad's a squirrel?'

'Think about it, Lenny . . .'

'Oh, your dad has the tattoo.'

'Exactly. Talking of dads, I thought you were meeting yours this evening?' I said, heading for the bedroom door so he'd get the hint.

He shrugged and sat down on my bed. 'Got caught up in a top-secret mission, didn't he?'

'Did he? That's a shame. Maybe we should chat about all this tomorrow, when we're somewhere else that isn't . . . here.'

'He's had a lot of really important missions recently.' Lenny gave a big sigh and plumped up my pillow like he was about to make himself comfortable.

'Well, you know spies – always busy. And, talking of busy, I'm actually up to my eyeballs too –'

'You were just lying around on your bed when I got here.'

'Lenny,' I said, maybe too forcefully, 'I don't want you here.'

Lenny looked as if I'd shot him in the stomach.

'It's not that I don't want *you*,' I said, pulling him up. 'I just don't want you *here*. Do you understand?'

Lenny nodded, then tilted his head and said, 'Actually, no, I'm not sure I do.'

'Look, let's talk tomorrow,' I said, dragging him along the landing and down the stairs, stepping over the dogs, Scooby and Doo.

I managed to get him all the way to the front gate before he stopped and said, 'Agatha, is everything OK?'

I glanced back at my house. 'Everything's fine.

I'll see you at school, all right?'

He nodded, stuffed his hands in his pockets and started off up the road.

'And, Lenny,' I shouted after him, 'I'm sorry about your dad!'

He gave a small nod. 'Me too.'

I sat down on the sofa that's in the front garden and let out a big, big sigh.

So now Lenny knew where I lived, and I didn't know how I felt about that.

I didn't know how he felt about that either.

The next day at school, Lenny came bounding up to me as I was hanging my coat on its peg. I didn't have time to feel awkward about what had happened the night before because, before I could open my mouth, he said, 'You'll never guess what I've just seen! Follow me!'

He led me to the library.

Outside the door, he pressed his finger to my lips for me to be quiet and then to his own lips.

I'm not sure why he needed to do both, but there you go.

Carefully, he opened the door, just a crack.

'Minerva Automated Librarian System will have this place modernized and working efficiently in next to no time!'

It was Ms Stranglebum. 'I'll just plug in the first few docking ports and then I can begin the demonstration.'

Mr Pardon came into view and said in quite a huffy manner, 'I'll have you know, madam, that this library works incredibly efficiently already. Dr Errno, I'm sure you'll see this new system will be a stupendous waste of money.'

'Mr Pardon, we have had this discussion several times. This is the way forward for Little Strangehaven Primary. I have made my decision and will not be persuaded otherwise. I'm sorry you don't like it, but perhaps we could discuss another role within the school. Maybe photocopier operative?'

Mr Pardon made a noise like a spluttering

kettle. 'I have never been so insulted!'

'Perhaps we should see your demonstration, Pamela – I mean, Ms Stranglebum,' said Dr Errno smoothly. '*That* may change Mr Pardon's mind.'

Ms Stranglebum smiled and said, 'Of course.' Then, with Dr Errno's help, she lifted a big silver box on to the table. It had the Minerva owl logo on the side.

'Cool,' Lenny whispered. 'We're about to be the first pupils to see those laser-eyed, owl-robot librarians in action.'

'Lenny, it's not going to be robot owls!' I whispered back. *Honestly!*

Ms Stranglebum unclipped the lid of the box, releasing a hiss of air.

'We keep them in hermetically sealed pressurized containers until they're ready for use,' she explained.

She pressed a button, and something large, metal and egg-shaped rose out of the box. A red button on the top flashed like a beacon.

'Ready, Dr Errno?' she said, raising an eyebrow.

'Very.'

Lenny squished his face further into the gap in the door. Even Mr Pardon looked intrigued.

Ms Stranglebum pressed the button and it flashed from red to purple. The metal egg opened and – to my absolute disbelief – three objects were revealed.

'Laser-eyed robot owls!' Lenny gasped. 'What did I tell you?'

'You have got to be kidding me!' I said, because in what world is Lenny right over me?

'Incredible,' Dr Errno said, his eyes almost as wide as his nostrils.

Ms Stranglebum placed the three robot owls into their docking ports and said, 'What we really could do with is a child.'

I dived out of the way as Dr Errno made his way towards the door, but Lenny was so completely enthralled by the robot owls, he didn't move.

Before I could do anything, Dr Errno had opened the door and Lenny was lying face down on the library carpet.

'That one will do nicely,' Ms Stranglebum said. 'What's your name?'

Lenny jumped to his feet and said, 'Lenny.'

'Well, Lenny, you're a very lucky boy. You're going to be our first test subject. Would you mind taking a seat there?' Ms Stranglebum motioned to a chair next to Mr Pardon's desk.

I thought Lenny might try to make an excuse, but he just said, 'OK!'

Ms Stranglebum pushed down on the head of one of the shiny metal owls. Its eyes flicked open and glowed red.

Lenny said, 'Cool!' as the thing flew over and landed on his head.

'This is the exciting bit,' Ms Stranglebum said. 'The automated librarian will now scan the child's brain to determine the best reading material. This part usually takes around ten to fifteen minutes –'

Without warning, the bird flew off Lenny's head and over to the bookcases. Ms Stranglebum blinked. 'Goodness, that was quick.'

Mr Pardon watched in stunned silence as the librarian-owl returned with a book in its beak and dropped it into Lenny's lap.

'Remarkable,' Dr Errno said.

Ms Stranglebum smiled. 'Minerva automated librarians are programmed to select reading material appropriate to the level of the pupil.'

'"My First Words?" But I know loads of words!' Lenny said to the owl. 'Don't you have anything funny? Funny books are the best.'

The owl ignored him and flapped back to its docking station.

Ms Stranglebum turned to Dr Errno. 'Our Minerva librarians are programmed to only select worthy and educational reading material. The librarian has determined this particular child requires practice in more . . . basic skills.'

'*Remarkable*,' Dr Errno said again, without

tearing his eyes away from Ms Stranglebum. He wafted a hand in Lenny's direction. 'You may go.'

Lenny came out of the library, colouring book in hand, and we wandered off towards our classroom.

'What do you think?' I said to him.

'I'm torn, Agatha. While flying robot-owl librarians *are* pretty cool, I am not completely wowed by their book recommendations.'

'No, I meant, do you think Minerva has anything to do with the **SHIVERS**? Maybe they have the technology to create the Strangeness. But why . . .?'

I really wasn't concentrating on anything Miss Happ was saying during our lesson on place value. I didn't even notice when Ernie got one of his counters stuck up his nose. My brain was far too busy trying to figure out whether Ms Stranglebum and her librarian owls had anything to do with the **SHIVERS** or if Dr Errno remained my prime suspect.

I was still pondering when the bell rang for break. I wandered along, mentally going over the events leading up to each of the **SHIVERS**, which wasn't easy because Lenny was gabbling on about his top three methods to retrieve objects from nasal cavities.

'Lenny!' I grabbed his arm as a brainwave hit. 'If Minerva *does* have something to do with the **SHIVERS**, Ms Stranglebum might be working with Dr Errno. And the fact that she's here in the school as we speak means they could start the next **SHIVER** at any moment. Which means we have to be ready to catch them in the act!'

'Oooh, what's it going to be this time?' Lenny said, sort of missing the point. 'You don't really think our heads might inflate to the size of that beast guy, Will's, and then explode, do you?'

'Who? What? Look, how am I supposed to know? Our heads could blow up, or it might start raining inside, or we might all grow monkey tails! I. JUST. DON'T. KNOW! What we need to think about is how to –'

But, before I could finish explaining, the next **SHIVER** struck!

'You are kidding me!' I said. 'Quick, we need to act!'

'Monkey tails! You think?' Lenny shouted excitedly, immediately starting to spin in circles, which was not exactly the action I had in mind.

'What are you doing?' I asked, not completely sure I wanted to hear the answer.

'I'm trying to check if I *am* growing a monkey tail because I've always thought it would be a pretty cool thing to have. You know, to swing through trees and suchlike.'

Before I could press him on what the 'suchlike' was, Lenny went from turning in circles to hurtling towards the ceiling.

Lenny was airborne! He was floating!

A nanosecond after Lenny, I shot upwards too, and thwacked into the ceiling with such force that a large chunk of plaster dropped to the floor.

My tummy did a giant wibble – it was a *long* way down. Not that I'm afraid of heights, you understand. It's falling from them I have a problem with. I was still a bit dazed when Lenny crashed into me.

'We're flying!' he said. '*Wheee!*'

'We are not *flying*, Lenny. We're pinned to the ceiling.'

'I'm like a bird!'

'You're not at all like a bird. We are literally just stuck on the ceiling.'

'I feel so free!'

'Lenny, you've got your head in my armpit.'

He wiggled out. 'This is the best thing EVER!'

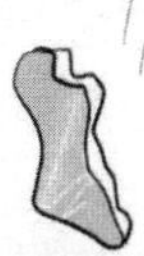

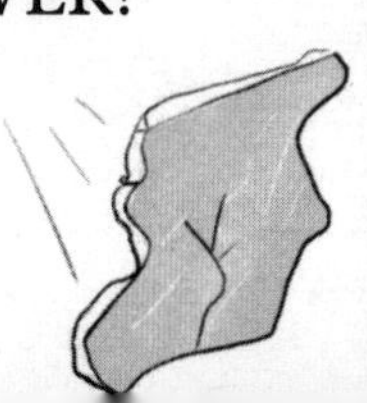

'Well, it won't be if the **SHIVER** comes again and we plummet to the ground.'

Lenny looked at me in horror.

'This is the WORST thing EVER!' he wailed. 'Oh, matzo balls! We're going to die! I want to get down! Why couldn't I just have had a tail!'

'I don't think we can *get down*. It's like we've lost all our gravity.'

'Well, I want it back!' he wailed. 'I didn't realize how much I liked it before! I'm sorry, gravity. I won't ever take you for granted again!'

'Lenny, stop freaking out!'

'But what shall we do?' Lenny said, flapping about wildly and spinning in circles.

'Well, we can't go after Stranglebum and Errno now. We'll need to air-swim to somewhere where it'll be safe to drop.'

'Air-swim?'

'Yeah, like regular swimming, but in the air.'

'But I haven't even got my ten-metre swimming badge!' Lenny wailed again.

Frankly, there was far too much wailing going on for an assistant spy-detective.

'I was swimming so fast my trunks slid off and I tried pulling them back up and then I swallowed water and started coughing and then my trunks came completely off and the whole class was laughing and –'

'Lenny! Calm down! You don't need a swimming badge and you aren't wearing trunks. We're just air-swimming.'

'OK . . . OK . . . I can air-swim.' He didn't sound that confident. 'Can't be too difficult. I can do this. Where are we going?'

'How about the gym? We could float above the crash mats and, when the **SHIVER** returns, we'll have a nice soft landing.'

'That's a good idea. Follow me!' Lenny said, then took a deep breath and began thrashing about. His arms circled wildly and every so often he'd lift his head and take another huge gulp of air. He was going absolutely nowhere.

'Lenny,' I said, tapping him on the shoulder, 'what are you doing?'

'What you told me to do! Air-swimming to the gym. I didn't realize it was so far. Let's keep going – the **SHIVER** may come back at any moment.'

He took another huge breath, stuck his head down and started flapping his arms about again.

I grabbed hold of his elbow. 'Lenny!'

He stopped and glared at me. 'What is it with you and my elbows?!'

'Lenny, can you swim *at all*?'

'Er, obviously. You've seen my synchronized swimming certificate.'

'It's just that your front-crawl technique is not really translating into air-swimming very well. Perhaps you should try another stroke? Or maybe

I could tow you?'

'I'm doing fine, thank you very much,' he said, a bit stroppily.

'Oh really?'

'Yes, *really*!' He took another giant breath, his cheeks flushing red.

'You know you don't need to hold your breath for air-swimming because we're literally swimming in air?'

His cheeks deflated. 'Of course.'

Then off he went, doing a head-up doggy-paddle like a very snooty Snoopy, which isn't really proper air-swimming in my book, but at least he was moving forward this time.

CHAPTER 14
LENNY

It was my moment to be super brave, even though we were floating high up off the ground. I had to be as courageous as I could, to try and make Agatha feel better. She was clearly terrified.

As was the whole school.

We swam into absolute mayhem. There were kids floating everywhere, screaming and crying. There were teachers floating everywhere, screaming and crying. There were dinner servers floating out of the dining room, screaming but not crying because they're made of tougher stuff than teachers.

The teachers were trying to take control of the situation, shouting instructions, but that wasn't easy while they were screaming and crying.

There were children bumping into each other and off the cracked ceiling. There were children upside down. Rahul was clinging to a ceiling light with his feet, like a terrified bat.

It was total and utter *chaos.*

Probably because none of them had mastered the art of air-swimming as I had.

Swimming through the air, it turns out, is just like swimming in a pool, except you can't do a wee without people noticing.

I'm afraid to say that I learned this the hard way.

I was happily doggy-paddling along when instinct took over and it just happened. It splashed on to the ground beneath me, making a pleasant splattering sound, like rain on our conservatory roof.

I'm not proud to say that there were two Reception children hovering underneath me at that unfortunate moment who also got a bit of a sprinkling.

Agatha gave me a look that I think meant she understood, and that, if she hadn't been so terrified, she might have done the same thing.

After I'd finished, I continued swimming, and made it to the big double doors at the end of the corridor.

'This way!' I said, and I pushed them open and swam through.

'No! *Not* that way!' Agatha shouted. But she was too late, so it was really *her* fault that I floated outside, into the big blue sky.

I heard her yell after me, 'Oh, so *that* door you can open!', which was neither kind nor supportive.

Being outside and without my gravity was not an ideal situation.

I felt myself floating upwards. Higher and higher I went, totally not screaming about the thought that I might be on my way to Mars.

Even with my super-brain, I couldn't figure out what to do to stop myself from exiting Earth's atmosphere. Luckily, I felt a hand grab my foot.

It was Agatha. She was still floating, but was clinging on to one of the horrible-looking stone gargoyles with one hand, and my foot with the other. She had also let the door shut behind her, which was very amateurish of her.

She looked like she was struggling.

'Can't hold . . . on . . . much longer,' she gasped.

Just as I was thinking how it would have been a lot better if I was the one holding on, because I was much stronger, Agatha's hand slipped and she let go of the gargoyle.

Typical.

As we both started floating off into the wide blue yonder, I think I heard Agatha screaming, but I couldn't be *one hundred per cent* certain who it was.

We began to bob across the playground. I was still trying to be courageous, but it was hard with Agatha thrashing about on the end of my leg.

For some reason, she grabbed hold of a basketball post as we drifted over it.

'What do you want that for?' I shouted.

'It's an anchor!'

'Er, Agatha, that's not an anchor – it's a basketball post.'

'Lenny! It's an anchor in that it's stopping us from floating off into outer space.'

Agatha's anchor held us for a moment, but the pull of our antigravity was quite strong, and slowly we started to drag it across the playground.

The 'anchor' then **SMASHED** through a fence and into the staff car park, straight towards a very shiny car with the number plate MIN3RVA 666.

The owner wasn't going to be happy because we dragged that basketball post right over the top of the flashy red paintwork, leaving a massive dent and a lot of scratches.

'Look what your anchor's done now, Agatha!' I said.

She didn't let go, though, but held on tight, and we dragged that basketball post all the way through the car park, right across the pet cemetery where all the school pets are laid to rest (RIP, Gingerbum Snugglepuffin, Year Three hamster), out to the school's conservation area and into the pond.

It was here that we felt the **SHIVER** again. Which was good in that when we plummeted from the sky we did not land on hard ground, but bad due to the fact that we ended up in scummy pond water.

As if that wasn't enough, I got caught in some treacherous pondweed, which tangled round my legs, so I was unable to swim to safety. It was dragging me down and NOBODY could have escaped from it. It really wasn't safe to have that stuff in a school pond.

To be fair to Agatha, she made up for not warning me about floating out of the door by helping me pull myself free, and, though I was exhausted from my deathly struggle, I managed to drag myself to safety.

CHAPTER 15
AGATHA

There was quite an odd atmosphere when we got back for afternoon registration. We arrived at the same time as Rahul, who was getting a right telling-off from Mr Wiener the cleaner for being found dangling from a school light. Apparently, it had taken quite some time to coax him down on to the stepladder.

He wasn't the only one who'd required assistance. Quite a few children were discovered in unusual places – some were perched on top of cupboards, others swinging from the stage curtains, and several were found clinging to window ledges.

This was all probably the reason behind the

first message Miss Happ read out after she'd taken the register.

'There is to be a total ban on the game known as *The Floor is Lava*, commencing immediately,' she said, eyeballing everyone in the room. 'School property is *not* to be clambered upon.'

It was bad timing for Ernie to call out for help to get down from the top of Miss Happ's stationery cupboard.

Once Ernie was back in his seat and Miss Happ had growled at him for messing about, she delivered her second message.

'The next thing I wish to discuss,' she said, 'is altogether more serious. An act of vandalism has been reported. To a visitor's car. A *very important* visitor. If anyone here knows what happened, *or* why there is a basketball post in the school pond, speak now.'

Everybody stayed silent.

At this moment, Dr Errno and Ms Stranglebum appeared in the doorway. He looked very, very angry and her left eyebrow was twitching rapidly.

'I am going round the classes,' Dr Errno said, 'to discover who is responsible for the damage to Ms Stranglebum's vehicle.' He lifted his chin and pointed his hypno-nostrils directly at us. 'Does anyone here have anything to say?'

The silence continued. Ms Stranglebum's other eyebrow started twitching.

'We are incredibly fortunate to have Ms Stranglebum in our school. On Monday, we shall be unveiling a library system that will revolutionize your learning here at Little Strangehaven Primary, and I am deeply ashamed that something like this could have happened. If you know anything, speak up now!'

Lenny and I kept quiet, but Jordan Wiener said, very unhelpfully, 'Little Puke – I mean *Lennox* – and Agatha might.'

'We don't know anything,' I hissed at him.

Jordan tilted his head and gave a smug smile. 'Then why are you both soaking wet?'

Miss Happ said, 'Agatha Topps, if you *do* know something, you should tell Dr Errno now, or you'll be in serious trouble.'

'I'm afraid I can't help you,' I said and flashed Dr Errno my most innocent smile. It's one I've practised in the mirror specifically for interrogations like these.

'Agatha, are you sure?' Miss Happ pressed.

A good spy-detective never buckles under pressure. 'Quite sure,' I said.

Miss Happ turned her attention to Lenny.

'Lenny, do you know what happened?'

Unfortunately, Lenny is not made of such strong stuff and he cracked immediately under the combination of Miss Happ's fierce gaze, Ms Stranglebum's twitching eyebrows and Dr Errno's flaring nostrils.

'Agatha was having a few issues with her gravity so she grabbed the basketball post to use as an anchor *apparently*, and then she dragged it over a shiny red car and threw it into the pond!'

'What?!' I shouted.

I'd only done it to stop Lenny floating off into space! I began to wonder if I should have let him take his chances with the Martians. I couldn't believe my ears!

I don't think Dr Errno could either because he blinked twice and then said, 'We do not appreciate people wasting our time with lies, Mr Tuchus. You and Miss Topps are to go to lost property and find

yourselves some dry clothes. I'm not having you sitting here in a puddle of dishonesty.'

We shuffled out of the classroom while Ms Happ read out the rest of the messages and Dr Errno steered Ms Stranglebum down the corridor, asking her exactly how much her car had cost. *Hmmm.* They seemed awfully cosy.

On the way out of school later, wearing a pair of trousers that were too short and a jumper that was too big and a frown that was just right, I took a deep breath and put my worries about home to one side. This investigation was too important, and besides I still felt bad about kicking Lenny out the night before. That was no way to treat an assistant.

'Lenny, I think you should come over to my house for a sleepover tonight because I have a plan,' I said very quickly, before I had a chance to change my mind.

He stopped outside the school gates and grinned at me. 'What, like a play date?'

'No, not at all like a play date. Spy-detectives don't have play dates, Lenny. We're going on a *mission*.'

'OK! That'll get me out of my music lesson. My mum wants me to try learning the kazoo. But I might still tell her it's a play date. I'm not sure how she'd feel about me going on a mission, especially after a busy week at school.'

I shrugged. 'Do what you have to do. And, by the way, I'm still annoyed about what you said to Miss Happ about it being all my fault.'

'I wasn't the one battering cars with basketball posts, Agatha,' Lenny said with a shrug.

I didn't have a comeback strong enough to show how I was feeling, so I settled for a massive huff and I think he got the picture.

I walked with Lenny back to his house. His mum was standing on the doorstep, waiting for him.

'My angel, Lenny-Loo-Loo, how was your day? Tell me all about it!'

We sat round the kitchen table and Mrs Tuchus gave us some bags of crisps and bourbon biscuits, which I snuck into my pocket to take home to share with my brothers and sisters.

I got the impression that, like me, Lenny might not have been on many play dates because, when he asked if he could stay at mine, his mum actually whooped with joy.

'It's so nice,' she said to me, taking my face in her hands, 'that Lenny-Loo-Loo has a friend.'

I did *not* know where to look!

Then she reminded Lenny that his dad would be coming over the next morning, to make up for the fact that he'd not shown up the day before (or the time before that), and so Lenny needed to be back by 10 a.m. on Saturday at the latest.

We went upstairs so he could pack his overnight bag.

'Bring some dark clothes,' I told him. 'And a torch.'

'What do I need a torch for?'

It wasn't the cleverest question, but I answered it anyway. 'To see in the dark. Oh, and if you have one, pack a balaclava.'

'I don't have a balaclava,' Lenny said. 'But I can improvise.'

He rummaged around in his drawers some more, threw a few things into his bag and zipped it up. He then pointed his fingers at me, like he thought they were guns or something, and said, 'All righty! This play date is on!'

'Mission! We're on a *mission*, Lenny. To find out what's going on with these **SHIVERS** once and for all.'

CHAPTER 16
LENNY

Agatha's dad was hanging up the washing when we arrived. He had one baby strapped to his chest and another strapped to his back. He came over to introduce himself to Mum and then said, 'Welcome to mayhem, Lenny.'

'Are you sure it's OK for Lenny to stay? You look like you already have your hands full,' Mum said.

'One more kid in this house isn't going to make a difference,' said Mr Topps with a grin. 'The older ones pretty much look after themselves.'

Mum made a wobbly noise, gave me a really tight hug and said, 'Call me if you need anything. I'll miss you, poppet!'

She hesitated before getting in the car and then shouted at me as I walked up the path, 'I LOVE YOU, my angel!'

'Gah! I love you too,' I said back, just to get rid of her, and she finally drove off.

Agatha's dad said, 'Your mother's upstairs, trying to catch up on some sleep. These two kept her up all night. So try your best to keep the noise down, and do me a favour and put the stuff on the draining board away.'

The door to Agatha's house was wide open and when we walked in the first thing that struck me was the noise. It was the sound of lots of kids shouting and laughing. No way could anyone be sleeping through that.

Her brothers and sisters came hammering down the stairs and Agatha introduced them as they raced past.

'That's Tom and George, the older twins. They're seven and into football and bugs.'

'Hi,' I said.

COLOUR
TOM

'And there's Iris, who's three, and Mavis – she's four – and Davey's five. They mainly like spaghetti hoops and piggyback rides, and they think anyone who burps is hilarious.'

I burped my name for them and they fell about laughing and then toddled off.

'You saw the babies already, Nigel and Trevor.'

Agatha's two small, yapping dogs then bolted along the hallway. The bigger one attacked my trainers and then tried to grab my special balaclava out of my bag. The other one did a very long wee against the banisters.

'Don't mind Doo – he's always stealing things that aren't his. He brings them back eventually. And Scooby's got a bit of a bladder problem. We tried to put him on medication, but it was too expensive . . . But anyway . . . that explains the smell, and –' she kicked another *very* full washing basket out of the way – 'just ignore all the mess.'

Agatha said all that very quickly and looked quite embarrassed. I don't know why. It wasn't her piddling on the banisters.

I actually didn't mind her incontinent and criminal dogs, or the mess. OK, it wasn't the fanciest place, but at least there was a lot going on.

A bleary-eyed woman in a Winnie-the-Pooh nightie came down the stairs, carrying *another* clothes basket.

'Mum, this is Lenny,' Agatha said.

'Lovely to meet you, Lenny,' she said through a yawn. Then she looked at the dirty washing. 'It's *never-ending*! But, as long as the love outweighs the laundry, we're doing OK, aren't we, kiddo?'

Agatha shrugged and blushed.

Mrs Topps smiled at her and said, 'So tell me, my beautiful firstborn, how are –' But then something outside caught her eye and she shouted, 'Tom, get that snail away from your brother's face!' and marched off into the garden.

'"How was school, Agatha? Did you have a good day, Agatha? Is everything OK, Agatha?"' Agatha muttered, which confused me for a moment before I realized she was saying the things she wanted her mum to ask.

Which were pretty much the same things I would have liked to have heard from my dad once in a while.

I followed Agatha into the kitchen, where I helped her put a load of plates and cups into the kitchen cupboards. Then we grabbed a couple of packets of crisps to take upstairs.

A few minutes later, we were eating salt-and-vinegar Hula Hoops in her room. Well – it wasn't exactly *her* room. She shared it with her brothers Tom and George. I couldn't quite work out where everybody slept because there was only one bunk bed.

'You're lucky to have such a big family,' I said, examining the Hula Hoops I'd placed on each of my fingers.

'Having a big family isn't always so great,' Agatha said quietly. 'I do love Tom and George and Iris and Mavis and Davey and Nigel and

Trevor, but that's a lot of kids and only two parents.'

'I bet you've always got people to play with, though. I've only got my mum and she's rubbish at wrestling. My dad's a bit better, when he remembers to show up.'

'Not much time to play when you're a spy-detective, Lenny,' Agatha said, and I wasn't sure if she was talking about my dad or herself.

'Still, nice to have people around, you know, to talk to and stuff.'

Agatha gave me a small smile. 'Yeah, I suppose. But because there's loads of us and, as Dad says, kids cost money, we can't afford many new clothes and things. And people at school – well, maybe that's why I've never had many friends over.'

Now that she mentioned it, her clothes did look a little scruffy. Her trousers had a rip and there was a patch on the elbow of her school jumper. I hadn't really thought about it before. I assumed it was just a look she was going for, to match her lopsided bunches.

'Well, I don't care,' I said, through a mouthful of Hula Hoops. 'I like you just the way you are.'

And then the most confusing and possibly actually the *worst* thing ever happened. Way worse than growing a beard or nearly floating to certain death.

Agatha jumped up and hugged me.

With absolutely NO warning whatsoever!

And then she stopped hugging me as suddenly as she'd started, and pushed me away, saying, 'What did you do that for?'

'Do what? YOU hugged ME!' I said, spluttering crisps at her.

'I most certainly did not!'

'You did. I was sitting here, in this spot, happily eating my snack, saying I didn't mind that you were poor and scruffy –'

'Scruffy?!'

'Sorry, maybe I thought that in my head, but the fact is *you* were the one who launched yourself at *me* with your great long waggly hugging arms!'

'Can we get professional and focus on the mission for a moment, please? And, for your information, my arms are a regular size for a child my age.'

'Fine,' I said, then very quietly muttered, because she needed to know, 'but it wasn't me doing all the unprofessional hugging.'

Agatha ignored my mutterings and got

organizational. 'Here's the plan. We're going to break in –'

'Break in?' I gasped. 'Where?'

'To school,' she said as if it was no big deal.

'Like criminals?'

'No, not like criminals. The complete opposite to criminals. We're the goodies – the heroes. We're trying to find out what's causing the **SHIVERS** before something *really* bad happens.'

I thought about it and decided I was actually OK with a bit of breaking in if it meant I was going to be a hero.

'OK, how's it going to work?'

'We're going to sneak into school and search around until we find what we're looking for.'

'Brilliant,' I said. 'Although what exactly are we looking for?'

Agatha said, 'The answer to what is going on at Little Strangehaven Primary!' in a tone that I did not appreciate.

So I said, 'And what *is* the answer to what's

going on at Little Strangehaven Primary, smarty-pants?'

And Agatha said, 'If we knew that, Lenny, we wouldn't have to break in and look for it.' Which I suppose was fair. But then she added, 'Honestly, sometimes it's not easy being the only professional member of a spy-detective team.'

Which was very *not* fair after ALL HER HUGGING earlier.

CHAPTER 17
AGATHA

I was sure that there would be some incriminating evidence at school linking Dr Errno, and possibly Ms Stranglebum, to the **SHIVERS**, but, if we were going to break in, it was crucial that Lenny was clear on the plan.

'It is very important we don't get caught,' I told him. 'So to avoid that we should –'

'Create a distraction!' he shouted.

I tilted my head.

'A distraction?' It wasn't the worst idea. I decided to hear him out. 'What did you have in mind?'

Except I don't think Lenny had *anything* in mind. I suspect he just shouted the first thing that came into his head because the next thing he blurted out was, 'I know! How about . . . How about . . . we . . . we set fire to the school? That would be distracting.'

'What?! NO! NO FIRE! Terrible idea!'

'Fine!' he said. 'What about if we . . . if we . . . release a flock of deadly scorpions to –'

'No!' I shouted again. 'I mean, where would we even get a *nest* of deadly scorpions from? Actually, never mind, don't answer! No deadly scorpions!'

'Killer robots with laser nipple-blasters?'

'I . . . I . . . I don't know what to say . . .'

Lenny beamed. 'Is that a yes I'm hearing for laser-nipple-bots?'

'Absolutely not!'

He did a big huff. 'Fine. I didn't think you'd be so lacking in imagination and now I'm completely out of brilliant ideas. Why don't *you* come up with a plan if you're so smart?'

'My plan, Lenny, if you'd let me finish, is that

we break into the school at *night*. Tonight, in fact.'

'At night? Won't it be dark?'

'Exactly! Which means we won't be seen, which removes any need for deadly scorpions or robots with nipple-lasers.'

'That's why you wanted me to bring a torch!'

'It is.'

'Does it matter that mine projects the Bat-Signal?'

'Only if he shows up and causes a fuss.'

'Oh, I can't guarantee he won't. We are breaking in, and that's exactly the sort of thing he usually tries to stop.'

'I think we'll be OK.'

After I'd made sure Lenny properly understood the plan, we had our tea of Pirate's Treasure with my family. All eleven of us – thirteen, if you include Scooby and Doo.

'Pirate's Treasure' means my mum or dad takes a really random selection of what's left in the cupboards and makes it sound exciting. It doesn't

work on me – nothing will ever make baked-bean soup followed by hot dogs mixed into rice pudding sound OK – but it does work on the younger kids, and Lenny too, actually.

After Lenny helped me do the washing-up (I think his house must have a dishwasher because he spent the whole time playing with the bubbles), we went up to my room. I gave Lenny my pillow so he could sleep on the camp bed. I was worried it might not be very comfortable because there's a big hole in it, but Lenny said it was the most comfortable camp bed he'd ever slept on, which made me feel like it might be OK.

I didn't know at the time that he'd never slept on any other fold-up bed.

I guess it didn't matter, though, because we weren't supposed to be going to sleep. We were planning on waiting until everyone *else* was asleep, then sneaking out.

It took ages for Tom and George to drift off in the top bunk they share. Mainly because Lenny got into a very long conversation with them about which insects they'd eat if they were starving.

Just before 11 p.m., I quietly climbed out of the bottom bunk and strapped on my utility belt containing all the things required for a mission, like rope, matches and a torch. I tiptoed over to Lenny and gave him a little poke.

'*Pssst*, Lenny, it's time.'

What I meant was that it was time for us to

become proper spy-detectives and break into school and solve the mystery of the Strangeness. Lenny, however, seemed to think it was time to stick his thumb in his mouth, roll over and say sleepily, 'No, I don't want to eat a slug.'

I gave him a firm shake. 'Wake up. It's time. And a slug isn't an insect.'

Well, the way he reacted, you would have thought I'd jabbed him with an electric cattle prod. He did not move quietly and slowly, as we'd discussed. He yelled and sat bolt upright with such force he caused the camp bed to spring shut, sandwiching him inside, his legs up by his earholes.

I considered leaving him there and carrying out the mission alone, but every spy-detective needs a hopeless sidekick. Besides, in my heart, I guess I wanted him with me, so I set him free and he crept off to the bathroom to get changed.

When he returned, wearing a pair of underpants on his head, I realized that maybe I should have left him in his camp-bed prison.

'Er, Lenny?'

'Yup?' he said with absolutely no indication that there was anything odd about his appearance.

'Is there a reason you have a pair of pants on your head?'

'Not pants, Agatha – this is my balaclava. Clever, eh? See how the leg holes make really good eye holes?'

I was about to tell him to take them off and stop being so ridiculous, but then I realized something: not everyone has a friend willing to break into school with a pair of underpants on their head.

'How do I look?' he said, giving a little twirl.

'I think you look perfect. Very spy-detectory.'

Because I really thought he did.

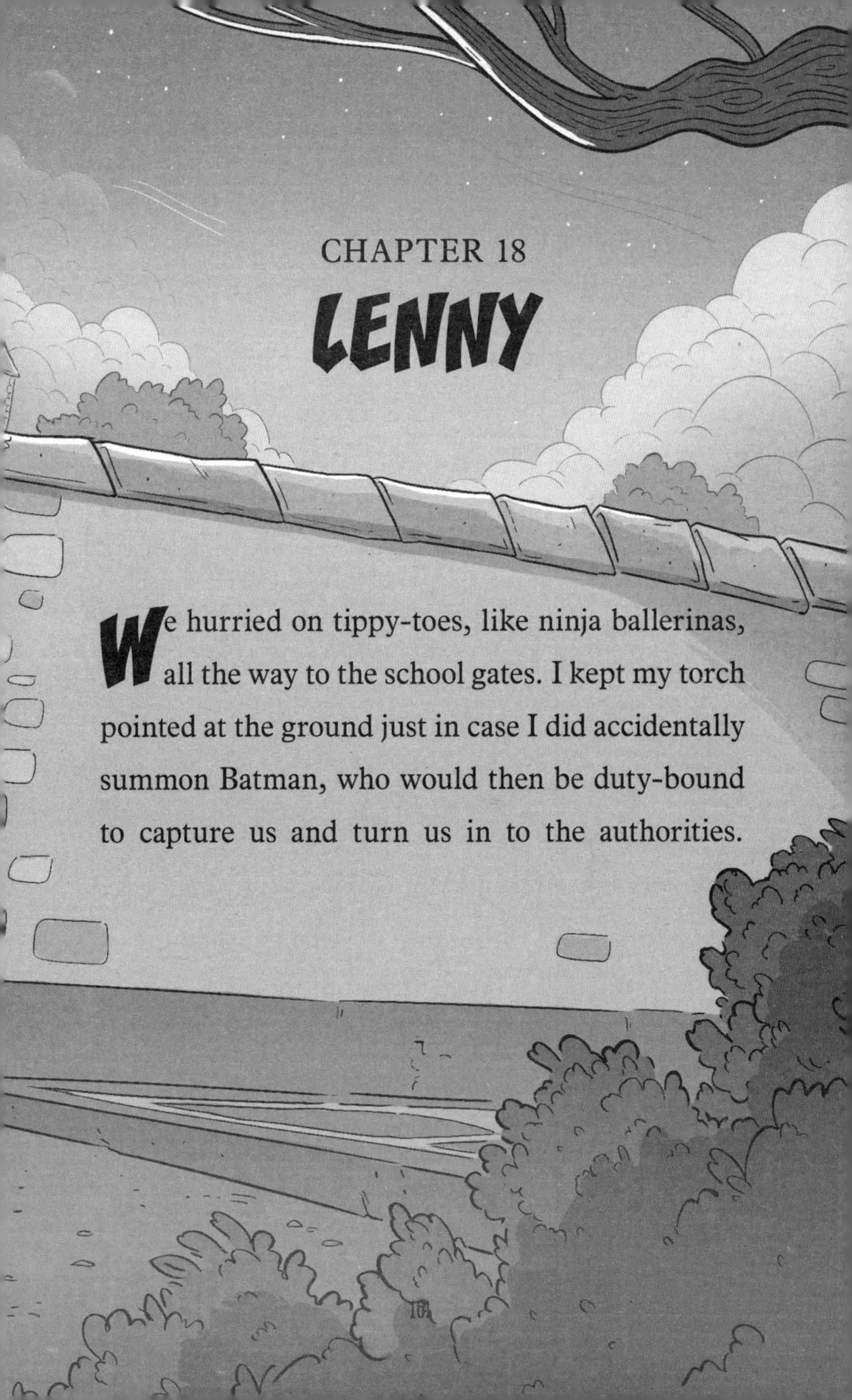

CHAPTER 18

LENNY

We hurried on tippy-toes, like ninja ballerinas, all the way to the school gates. I kept my torch pointed at the ground just in case I did accidentally summon Batman, who would then be duty-bound to capture us and turn us in to the authorities.

Look, I don't know if he really exists or not, but it's better to be safe than stopped by Gotham's greatest superhero.

When we got to the gates, they were locked.

Agatha peered through. 'Look, Stranglebum's car is still here! Maybe she's inside.'

'Or maybe she couldn't drive it after you bashed it with that basketball post.'

The school was extra spooky in the dark, looming over us, and it gave me a funny feeling in my bum just looking at it. Not that I'm afraid of the dark, mind you. I'm just apprehensive about a lack of lighting.

I pushed up my balaclava-pants (because my face was hot from all the tippy-toeing) and gave the gates a good rattle until Agatha shushed me.

'Dratballs,' she said. 'I thought we'd be able to slide underneath them.'

'There's no way we can fit under there.' I pointed at the three-centimetre gap under the gates. 'Bet you wish we'd brought those nipple-laser robots now, don't you? They would have been able to blast us through.'

'There has to be another way,' Agatha said, scanning all around, clearly struggling to come up with a plan.

'I have an idea!' I said, trying to think of one as I spoke. I always find it's best to start talking, even if you don't know what you're going to say, because your mouth puts your brain under pressure. It never fails. It's what got me to laser-nipple bots after all.

'Perhaps we could use some sort of cannon and fire me over the top? Or maybe we could find a trebuchet and catapult me in, like they did in medieval times?'

'All . . . *ideas*, Lenny,' Agatha said, clearly impressed. 'But maybe we should consider a less dangerous approach? And I currently have neither cannon nor trebuchet to hand.'

More evidence of Agatha's startling lack of planning.

'We could dig an underground tunnel with a ginormous drill?' I suggested. 'Or . . . or . . . blast the gates off with dynamite!'

'No, Lenny.'

'I'm telling you, Agatha, dynamite will get those gates open, no problemo. Do you have any in your utility belt?'

'No, I did not bring my dynamite with me this time,' she said, which was *another* big failing on her part, but I didn't point it out because I'm gallant like that.

'Perhaps we could climb over?' she suggested. 'But it's pretty high and I don't like the look of those spikes at the top. We'd have to be careful.'

'Careful is my middle name.' I stuck my torch into the back of my trousers and began to scramble up one of the gates like a squirrel monkey. 'And so is . . . Supreme Climber.'

I think I'd made it quite far up (I couldn't be sure because I had my eyes closed) when Agatha tugged my elbow and said, 'Lenny, what are you doing?'

'I'm climbing over the gate.'

'I've seen ducks climb better than that!'

Which was a lie because everyone knows ducks only climb trees, not gates.

'Don't put me off,' I hissed. 'I don't want to fall and rupture my spleen. Whatever that is.'

'You're about thirty centimetres off the ground, so I think your spleen – which is responsible for filtering old red blood cells, by the way – is quite safe.'

That couldn't be right. I'd been climbing for ages. I had to be higher than that. I opened my eyes to check.

'What trickery is this? Maybe the Strangeness has made the gates unclimbable?' I said. And then they swung open with me still clinging to the bars.

'Come on in,' Agatha said from the other side, and gave a little bow.

'Hey! How did you get there?'

'I climbed over. And pressed the buzzer to unlock them.'

I stood there for a moment, looking at the top of the gates, then back at Agatha, then at the top of the gates again.

'That was some top-notch spy-detectoring there, Agatha!'

'You just wait, Lenny. There's loads more where that came from,' she said and started legging it up the long driveway.

I chased after her, pretending she was faster than me, and thinking about how cool it was that I was working with such an excellent assistant.

CHAPTER 19

AGATHA

All the doors to the school were locked, but thanks to my special spy-detective skills, which I never turn off, I knew another way in.

There's a small window in one of the classrooms with a broken latch that no one had ever got round to fixing. I noticed it during one particularly unfascinating lesson on rocks and stored the information in my memory banks.

I gave Lenny a leg-up and he grabbed hold of one of the stone gargoyles set into the wall and pulled himself through the window. He landed on the floor with a very un-spy-detective-like *whoomph*.

I climbed up and dropped down after him,

making zero noise, like a cat in the night, you might say.

'We're in,' Lenny whooped. 'High five!'

'Shh! No high fives during a mission. We need to stay quiet. Do not make a sound.'

Honestly!

'Roger that,' Lenny said, and pulled his pants back down over his face.

'Let's go. I want to check out Dr Errno's office first. That's our best bet to find out whether it *is* him who's behind the **SHIVERS**, if Ms Stranglebum is involved, and how they're doing it.'

'Roger that,' Lenny said again. Then he added, 'Sounded very spy-detective-like then, didn't I?'

'Yes, very, Lenny. And you look very spy-detective-like too, in your own way.'

He grinned at me from behind his balaclava-pants, his eyes peeping out through the leg holes.

Quietly, I crept across the classroom, using the professional spy-detective slinking technique to minimize noise and visibility.

In the corridor, I turned back to check Lenny was keeping up. 'What are you doing?'

'I'm copying you *obviously*!' he whispered.

'Lenny, I'm *slinking*. I have absolutely no idea what you're doing.'

'I'm slinking too.'

'But what's with all the flappy arm and leg action? You look like an octopus. That's not slinking, that's *squidding*.'

Really, I blame myself. I should have dedicated more time to training him.

'Just try not to knock anything over with those flailing limbs of yours,' I whispered, and set off down the corridor again, only to hear Lenny say, in a very whiny voice, '*Just try not to knock anything over with those flailing limbs of yours.*'

I paused. 'I sound nothing like that!'

'*I sound nothing like that!*' Lenny said in the same whiny voice.

'Lennox! Stop messing about! We need to stay completely focused and alert during a mission, so we can react if something happens.'

And then something did happen.

We both felt it. The familiar electric crackle in the air. I saw Lenny's eyes widen behind his underpant-balaclava.

'Something like the **SHIVER**?' he said with a gulp.

'Yes, something just like that.'

CHAPTER 20
LENNY

Agatha and I stood absolutely still and completely silent while we waited to find out what the **SHIVER** would bring this time.

'Don't panic . . . don't panic . . .' she kept saying.

I should have a word with her about that, because telling someone not to panic has the EXACT opposite effect.

I tried my best to stay calm and in the spy-detective zone, despite Agatha not helping the situation at all. And I was doing well, thank you very much.

Until I heard it. A sort of tapping, scratching sound.

Agatha and I both looked up.

'What *is* that?' she said in a very wibbly-wobbly voice quite similar to the one my mum used when the plastic dinosaur she didn't know I'd swallowed appeared in the loo.

The scratching grew louder. It was definitely coming from the floor above.

'I have no idea,' I said in a very brave-sounding voice.

Agatha cupped her ear. 'It sounds like an army of scorpions scuttling across the floor.'

This could have been the time for me to point out that we might have had our *own* army of deadly scorpions if she'd agreed to my diversion plan. But I didn't because I'm not one to say, 'I told you so.'

The scuttling noise grew louder still, until it passed right above us – towards the stairs.

'Whatever it is, it'll be with us any minute now,' Agatha whispered.

My bum did that quivery thing where it went out and in a couple of times.

The sound of skittering footsteps spilled down the staircase.

I drew a very long breath and braced myself to do battle with whatever was coming for us, but Agatha pulled me by the elbow (of course) into a classroom and we hid behind the door.

She slapped her hand over my mouth, and said, 'Stop screaming,' which was completely unnecessary because I wasn't the one who was screaming. She was. The scream I could hear was far too high-pitched to be coming from me.

Through the crack in the door, we watched in horror as a shoal of *creatures* came stomping down the stairs.

They stopped at the bottom, grunting and groaning, steam coming in puffs from their squat, fat noses. They were like an army of short goblins, completely grey from head to toe, even down to their bared teeth. The one at the front pointed a gnarled finger down the corridor and off they all went, their talons clattering across the wooden floorboards.

'What *were* they?' I breathed, when they were safely out of sight.

'I don't know. They looked familiar . . .'

'What do you mean, they looked familiar?'

'Come on,' Agatha said. 'Let's get to Dr Errno's office before they come back. We have to find out how this is happening.'

'Right, we're carrying on with the mission then? I had kind of figured, what with the weird army of grunting monsters, that we might come back another day?'

'Of course we're carrying on! A good spy-detective never abandons a mission. Besides, we're here now.' Agatha opened the door and peeked out. 'It's fine. The coast is clear and Dr Errno's office is in the opposite direction to the way those *things* went. Let's approach with caution, though. He's probably in school right now, maybe Stranglebum too, and they could be the cause of the **SHIVER**!'

I hesitated. I wasn't totally happy about running round the school with either those *things* or Dr Errno about.

'Come on, Lenny. Don't be scared. I'll protect you.'

I took a big step out of the classroom to show that I was not someone who needed protection.

'I am not scared. I'm here to protect *you*, Agatha.'

And then I saw it.

One of the monsters.

Standing right behind her.

And I'm not completely sure how it happened, but somehow I ended up in Agatha's arms.

CHAPTER 21

AGATHA

After Lenny had leaped into my arms, there was very little I could do but stand there, cradling him. I did consider throwing him at the ugly grey monster, but I don't think that would have helped so, eventually, I just dropped him.

And then we both stood there with no idea what to do other than stare at one of the most grotesque, yet strangely familiar-looking things I have ever seen.

It folded back its wings, crossed its gnarly hands on top of its little pot belly and licked its grey lips.

'Are you going to . . . going to . . . eat us?' Lenny asked.

'*Shh*, stop giving it ideas!' I angry-whispered.

The monster shook its head and a couple of pebbles dropped out of its ears.

'Och no! I dinnae want to eat ye!'

It bent down on its funny little legs, picked the stones up and examined them for a moment, before popping them into its mouth and gulping them down.

Then it gave a big grin, its teeth jutting up like a row of broken tombstones, and took a big bite out of the wall.

'What are you?' I asked. 'Are you –'

'Scottish? Aye!' it said, brick crumbs falling from its mouth.

'No, I meant are you an ogre?'

It stopped munching, did a burp way louder than either Lenny or I could manage, and said, 'No, I'm no' an ogre. I am Gregor. And I'm alive!'

Then it did this weird little celebration dance and waggled its hips from side to side.

'He seems like a happy little fella,' Lenny whispered and bent down to pick up a small stone. 'Not like those other ones.'

Lenny held out a slightly shaking hand. 'Here you go, Gregor, a tasty stone for you.'

Gregor grabbed the stone, threw it in the air, caught it in his wide-open mouth and swallowed it down with a massive gulp.

'Thank ye for that stony morsel o' deliciousness, big-eared one! Och, let us be clansmen!'

Lenny's hands shot to his face. 'Hey, I do not have big ears!'

'No, yer right! Ye dinnae have big ears.'

'That's better,' Lenny said.

'Ye have the most enormous ears I've ever seen! They remind me o' great flappy sails and are surely the envy of all the land!'

'You're the one with the big ears!' Lenny shot back.

'Thank ye!' Gregor beamed. 'But ma ears are nothing compared to yer giant lugholes! I have seen many a pair pass beneath me, but none have stood out so proudly as yours!'

Then he dropped to the floor and started hoovering up more stones and a stray plimsoll.

I watched him, trying to figure out why he seemed so familiar. 'That's it!' I slapped my hand to my forehead. 'You're the gargoyle that sits over the front doors of the school.'

Gregor gave up trying to chew the rubbery trainer and spat it out.

'Aye, I've been sitting up there for over four hundred years.' He then did a couple of lunges and said, 'I'll tell ye this: it's nice to be up and aboot and stretching ma legs!'

'And when did you stop sitting up there?' I asked.

Gregor turned round, bent over again, swayed from side to side like he was stretching out his back, then looked up at us from between his legs. He had quite a lot of moss sprouting between his bum cheeks.

'After I felt the **SHIVER**, ma wee pals!'

It was then that I realized what had happened. I grabbed Lenny's elbow.

'That's what those other things are, Lenny. All of the school gargoyles! They've come alive!'

CHAPTER 22

LENNY

Agatha raced off down the corridor.

Personally, I was not one hundred per cent sold on the idea of running round a dark school full of gargoyles, but I couldn't let Agatha go alone. She might need someone strong and courageous if she got into trouble.

Gregor trotted along behind, panting and shouting things like, 'I am here for ye, ma wee brother!', 'Clansmen stick together,' and, 'Ye move at an impressive speed, great-eared one!'

'Agatha!' I shouted after her. 'What's the plan? And is this gargoyle going –'

'Gregor! Ma name is Gregor!' interrupted Gregor, the actually-getting-really-quite-annoying-now gargoyle.

'Is *Gregor* going to be with us the whole time?'

'Yes! He might have valuable information. And we're searching, Lenny. If Dr Errno is here, causing all this chaos, now's our chance to find him. Something tells me if we follow those gargoyles, he won't be far away!'

We rounded a corner, but slammed on the brakes when we came face to face with the rest of the gargoyles. They must have looped back round through the dining hall!

'Oh great,' I said, but I was being sarcastic.

The gargoyles were scuttling about on their knobbly little feet, chomping into whatever they could find.

One unfolded its wings, flew up to a strip light and started gobbling away at that.

Gregor rubbed his hands together, snapped off a door handle, broke it in two and handed a piece to me.

'Wrap yer gob around that, fellow clansman!'

Because Mum has always told me it's rude to turn down a gift, I took the handle and gave it a little lick so I didn't seem ungrateful.

Agatha snatched it out of my hand and threw it to the floor. 'Lenny! Stop licking door handles. Focus! We need to stop them. They're going to eat the school!'

I thought she was being a little hasty.

'Or maybe . . . we just leave them to it?' I said. 'Is no school really *such* a bad thing?'

Agatha turned and prodded me in the chest. 'Yes, Lennox! If you want to get on in life, you need a good education!'

She had the same scary glint in her eye that Mum gets whenever I say homework is a waste of time.

I held my hands up. 'Fine. We can stop the gargoyles eating the school if you really think we have to.'

'We do.' She nudged me forward. 'Go on then.'

'You want *me* to do it? I mean, I think this might be more your area of expertise.'

'Oh, for goodness' sake!' Agatha said, then took a step forward. She held her hands above her head and shouted, 'I command you all to stop eating the school building immediately!'

Either the gargoyles didn't hear her or they were ignoring her because they carried on happily chomping away. In fact, one of them took a bite out of the trophy cabinet.

'Ah well, you tried,' I said. 'Can't win 'em all.'

Agatha then stuck her fingers in her mouth and did a really loud whistle. As someone who struggles with whistling, I was very impressed.

And it worked, because all the gargoyles stopped eating and started glaring at us instead.

There was a definite change in atmosphere.

'They don't look very happy,' I said.

A few of the gargoyles started to growl. Then some of them began to lick their lips.

'Gregor,' I whispered, 'why are they looking at us like that?'

Gregor finished his mouthful of radiator and wiped the rust from his lips. 'Like what?'

'Like they want to eat us,' Agatha said quietly.

'Och no, ye wee walloper! Why would they want to eat ye when there's all this lovely brick aboot?'

One of the larger gargoyles sprang forward, landing very close to us. His stumpy legs were surprisingly powerful. He was even more horrible-looking than Gregor, with a chipped ear, a missing talon on his left foot and two black, unblinking eyes.

'Hello, fellow gargoyle,' Gregor said, stretching his arms wide. ''Tis a great day to be alive, is it not?'

The gargoyle leaned in very close to me, took two long, deep sniffs and said, *'Mmmmmmmm!'* like I was the best thing he'd ever smelled.

'Thank you,' I said. 'It'll be the rosemary, thyme and lemongrass shower gel I got from the last hotel I stayed at with my dad. Mum says it reminds her of roast chicken, but I quite like it.'

A long line of dribble slithered out of its jaws on to my shoes.

Before I could jump back, the gargoyle flicked out a long grey tongue and licked all the way up one arm and right across my face, leaving a line of silvery saliva that looked like a snail trail.

It was disgusting. And for some reason reminded me of when my Great-Aunt Joan kissed me at my cousin's bar mitzvah.

'Hey! That was rude!' I shouted, flicking the spittle off my arm. 'You can't just lick someone without asking!'

'Lenny . . . don't shout at the nice gargoyle,' Agatha said, which was not very supportive in my opinion.

'Nice?' I huffed. 'Since when is leaving a trail of slobber across someone's face *nice*?'

Agatha then started doing this weird glary thing with her eyes, and nodding her head, which I thought was strange until I saw that the rest of the gargoyles had stopped munching away on the school building and had formed a semicircle round us.

Old Mr Licky's horrible lips spread into a grin, revealing teeth that were much more pointy and dangerous-looking than Gregor's, and he let out a long *hissssssss*.

'Gregor, I really think this gargoyle is looking like he wants to eat us,' Agatha said again.

'Ah, you've nothing to worry aboot! Unless he's a Transylvanian gargoyle. Then yer in big trouble.'

The grinning, hissing gargoyle licked its sharp teeth and then spat, '*Te voi înghiți de tot!*'

'Och,' said Gregor, throwing his arms into the air. 'Now that's a wee bit o' bad luck.'

'What do you mean "bad luck"?' Agatha asked.

'They *are* Transylvanian gargoyles. Which means they might want to bite yer wee heads off after all.'

CHAPTER 23

AGATHA

Now, I've read a lot of survival books.

I know how to make a fire.

I know how to collect rainwater.

I even know how to capture and ride an antelope. In theory.

What I did not know is how to escape from a horde of Transylvanian gargoyles.

I cannot lie: the situation was not ideal. We were supposed to be getting to the bottom of the **SHIVERS**, but instead we were about to be eaten alive. It wasn't exactly how I saw the mission going when I was in the planning stages.

The gargoyles began to close in on us, one big mass of slobbering tongues and clattering talons.

Lenny, Gregor and I huddled together and started backing away.

'I don't want to be eaten by a Transylvanian gargoyle!' Lenny whimpered.

'Well, you should have thought about that before you made yourself smell like a freshly cooked roast chicken!'

I knew it wasn't really Lenny's fault we were about to be eaten, but I was cross about how everything was turning out and wanted to blame somebody that wasn't me.

The gargoyles moved closer still, drooling and growling and generally looking quite terrifying.

Gregor puffed up his little stone chest, balled his fists and said, 'Dinnae take one more step, or ye'll all be fer a lamping!'

I don't think Transylvanian gargoyles understand Scottish because they all sniggered and took another step.

I racked my brain for a plan. Something clever and brilliant that would get us out of the situation.

Perhaps it was time to put my negotiation training to use. We needed to act carefully. Cautiously.

Gregor, however, had decided that attack was the best approach. He swung his arm round and round in circles before hollering, 'Take that, ye contumacious scowderin' beastie!' and bopping the nearest gargoyle on the nose.

The gargoyle looked a bit stunned.

Lenny saw a chance and shouted, 'RUN!'

Running wasn't a bad idea because it was the only idea. So we turned and legged it. We charged back down the corridor, tripping and stumbling, with the Transylvanian gargoyles in hot pursuit the whole way.

Through the school we raced, up the large staircase, past the upstairs classrooms, where we did a full lap of the building, and then on to the main staircase that led down to the school reception area.

'To the open window!' I shouted as we thundered down the steps.

The gargoyles jumped off the landing and flew down to cut us off at the bottom.

So we ran back up the stairs.

They flew back up.

So we ran back down.

They flew back down.

So we ran back up . . .

You get the picture. It went on like this until Lenny called for a timeout.

Surprisingly, the Transylvanian gargoyles agreed. I think sitting about on the roof for 400 years meant they weren't at peak fitness.

As I bent over at the bottom of the stairs to catch my breath, though, I caught sight of the swoosh of a head teacher's gown at the far end of the corridor.

Dr Errno!

'Quick!' I shouted, and bolted after him. Gregor and Lenny chased after me and the Transylvanian gargoyles flew back downstairs and charged after us again.

I turned a corner and saw the door to the library swing shut.

'To the library!' I yelled.

'Is now *really* the best time for reading?' Lenny shouted.

Honestly, working with amateurs can be very trying.

Anyway, we hurried to the library, but before I could reach for the handle the door flew open and hit me right in the face.

I fell backwards on to Lenny, who fell backwards on to Gregor, who fell backwards on to the floor.

Someone jumped over us and raced off down the corridor, their black gown flapping behind them like wings.

'Is that . . . Batman?' Lenny said, looking down at his torch, his voice full of wonder.

'*Seriously*, Lenny? It's obviously Dr Errno.' I pulled him to his feet, but, by the time we were both standing, the Transylvanian gargoyles had blocked the corridor.

'He's getting away!' Lenny said.

'I know.'

'And the gargoyles want to eat us!'

'Yes, Lenny. That is an accurate assessment of the situation.'

'Well, I think you should do something about it!'

'Any ideas?'

LIBRARY

'Ooh yes!' Lenny said, his hand shooting into the air.

'*Really?*'

'I'm not sure. Let's see what falls out of my mouth.'

I wasn't hopeful.

'Do you have a stun gun?'

'No!'

'A lightsabre? They always look effective.'

'Lenny! This isn't *Star Wars*!'

'How about a giant ball to knock them over with, like in *Indiana Jones*?'

'No! Oh . . . hang on. Actually, that could work!'

I turned to Gregor and put my hands on his cold, stony shoulders. 'Will you fight, son of Scotland?'

Gregor puffed up his chest proudly. 'AYE! I will fight!'

'Good. We're going bowling!'

CHAPTER 24
LENNY

So I think we can all agree that it was my super-brain that saved the day. Well done, super-brain!

Under Agatha's instructions, Gregor curled up into a ball, like an oversized woodlouse.

'Now help me throw him,' she said to me.

Gregor uncurled himself. 'Throw me?'

'Yeah, at the gargoyles.'

'What?' Gregor shouted.

'It'll be fine, brave Gregor,' Agatha said. 'Now curl up!'

Gregor curled up again and we both grabbed hold of him.

'On three!' she yelled.

We swung him back and forth.

'One!'

'Arghhhhhhhh!'

'Two – be brave, Gregor!'

'I feel a wee bit sickkkkk!'

'Three! Godspeed, soldier!'

Gregor shouted, 'FOR FREEDOM!' and we released him.

Down the corridor he went, rolling, rolling, rolling. Faster and faster.

He went off to the left a little bit.

Then veered to the right.

Then he was on a
really good line,
heading right for
the middle
of the gargoyles.

But then he veered to the
right again and we thought he
might disappear into the staff
loos, but somehow

he got back on target
and smacked right into
the biggest gargoyle –
Old Mr Licky himself.

WALLLLLLOP!

Mr Licky went flying up into the air and crash-landed, taking out all the others!

'Strike!' I shouted.

The gargoyles lay strewn across the floor, groaning and moaning, and Agatha seized her chance.

She set off in the direction taken by Dr Errno (or possibly Batman), and I followed her in case my assistant needed me and not because I didn't want to be left on my own.

She ran over to Gregor, who was spinning round on his back like a tortoise on its shell, and plucked him up.

I heard her yell, 'Not so fast, Errno!'

And she bowled Gregor again, straight at him.

Gregor gave a wobbly wail. The poor little fella must have been quite dizzy at that point.

Still, he hurtled across the floor towards Dr Errno, wobbly-wailing the whole way. Dr Errno tried to zigzag, but Gregor bounced off a wall and took him out below the knees.

Dr Errno stumbled and something he was carrying flew up into the air.

Gregor then ricocheted off the opposite wall straight back towards us.

'WATCH OUT!' Agatha shouted, managing to hurdle over him, but I was deep in the spy-detective zone and too focused on what Dr Errno had accidentally hurled skywards.

I didn't jump. And the very hard stone bowling ball that was Gregor **WALLOPED** me right in the unmentionables.

A high-pitched squealing filled the corridor. I dropped to my knees. I fell on my side. Tears filled my eyes. I may have called out for my mummy.

I didn't move for several moments. Somehow, Gregor and I had ended up in some sort of gargoyle-Lenny bundle on the floor.

'It hurts!' I said.

'Aye,' Gregor whimpered. 'Let's rest a wee while.'

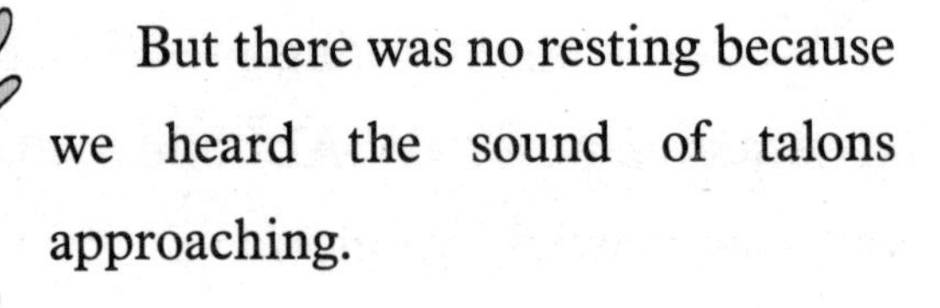

But there was no resting because we heard the sound of talons approaching.

The Transylvanian gargoyles were back on their feet and heading over to have a go at eating me again. *Why did I have to look so delicious?!*

I tried to untangle myself from all Gregor's knobbly gargoyle parts, but I couldn't really see what I was doing because I had my face stuck in his bum-moss, and he was wailing about needing to throw up, and I did not want to be covered in gargoyle vom, and I didn't know what Agatha was doing, and I was thinking that she wasn't a very good spy-detective AT ALL, and I was worrying about how much Mum would shout at me if a

Transylvanian gargoyle chomped my head off, and thinking that my dad *definitely* wouldn't bother to come and see a son without a head, and it was all a bit too much really . . .

But then I felt the **SHIVER.**

It pulsed through the air and passed right through me.

Immediately, the atmosphere changed.

Things suddenly felt very still.

Very calm.

I untangled myself from Gregor and got to my feet.

The Transylvanian gargoyles had completely disappeared. There was no trace that they had ever even been there. Dr Errno had vanished too, his footsteps echoing through the empty school.

And Agatha was standing at the end of the corridor, holding a massive book.

CHAPTER 25

AGATHA

As far as missions go, I would chalk up my first one with Lenny as a semi-success. While we did not capture Dr Errno and bring him to justice, we didn't get eaten by Transylvanian gargoyles either. And, although we weren't any closer to discovering what was actually causing the Strangeness, we did have our first proper clue in the form of a huge book.

After the Transylvanian gargoyles had all vanished, I took off my balaclava and turned the book over in my hands, running my fingers along the raised black lettering on the front cover.

'What *is* that?' Lenny limped towards me, removing the underpants from his face.

'The *Book of Chaos*,' I read out loud.

Open me . . .

'Who said that?' I yelped, looking around.

'Who said what?' Lenny asked, looking even more confused than normal.

'I thought . . . never mind.' I focused on the book. 'Dr Errno dropped it and ran off, and, when I closed it, the **SHIVER** came.'

Turn my pages . . .

I looked around again. 'Lenny, was that you?'

'Was that me what?'

'I could have sworn . . . Anyway, my spy-detectory instincts tell me this book may be the cause of all the weird things that are happening!'

See what lies within . . .

You must . . .

'I must what? Did you say something, Gregor?'

Gregor said, 'What? How? Who? Whenceforth?'

'Be honest, neither of you are saying anything, are you?'

They looked at me blankly so I handed Lenny the book and waggled my finger about in my ear.

'That's better. I'll continue.'

But I couldn't continue because Lenny said,

'Open you? Sure thing, lovely booky-wooky.' Then he gave it a kiss and went to open the cover.

Quickly, I knocked the book out of his hands on to the floor. 'No, Lenny!'

He scrabbled after it on all fours. Grabbed it, stroked it, SNIFFED it, then said, 'Must open my ickle booky-wooky!'

That's when I realized there was something seriously, *seriously* messed up about the *Book of Chaos*.

'Lenny, don't listen to it! I think the book is talking to you!'

I snatched it out of his hands and the feverish look disappeared from his eyes.

Open me, turn my pages . . .

'No thank you very much. Perhaps try a "please" next time,' I told the book and promptly stuffed it in my backpack where its tempting talk was muffled.

I turned to explain the situation to Lenny and Gregor.

'My mission findings are as follows. One: Dr Errno was our culprit after all. Two: it appears that the *Book of Chaos* REALLY wants us to open it. I believe it to be dangerous and therefore I should be the only one to handle it. Three: when I closed the book, it caused the second **SHIVER** and all the gargoyles disappeared. Hang on . . . How is *he* still here?' I said, pointing at Gregor. 'The second **SHIVER** should have turned him back to a regular gargoyle like the others.'

Gregor flexed his arms and said, 'Nothing regular aboot me, lassie!'

'What reason could there be for him to remain?' I wondered out loud.

Lenny's arm shot into the air. 'Oooh, I know! I know!'

I wasn't convinced he did, but I said, 'Go on, Lenny. What do you know?'

'He must be one of us! Remember Gregor said

he felt the **SHIVER** too? The three of us must share a connection!'

'I suppose it's not *completely* impossible . . .' I said, highly doubtful that anything could connect me, Lenny and a feisty Scottish gargoyle.

'It's *totally* possible!' Lenny said. 'Tell me, Gregor, do you have a mole named Bernard?'

'I'm afraid not, laddie. I'm blemish-free.'

'Matzo balls! I was sure that was it,' Lenny said, looking deflated.

'I've told you! It's not the mole thing, Lenny,' I said. 'But now is not the time for discussions. We need to get home before anything else happens. I want to take a closer look at the *Book of Chaos* and see if I'm right about it being the source of the **SHIVERS**.'

'What about Gregor?' Lenny said. 'We can't leave him here on his own.'

Lenny had a point. We couldn't have a gargoyle running round the school. That definitely wouldn't go unnoticed on Monday, especially if he kept taking bites out of the building.

'Oooh, please take me wi' ye! I want to see things! What lies beyond the school? Is it Scotland? Ma heart sings for the Highlands!'

'There's a Co-op and then a housing estate,' Lenny said.

'Sounds pure brilliant!' Gregor grabbed hold of my hands and looked up at me with big bloodshot eyes. 'Say I can tag along wi' ye?'

'Fine, you can come back to my house. But no eating the walls. Promise?'

Gregor nodded. 'I give ye ma word.'

It took longer than it should have done to get back to mine because Gregor kept trying to lick all the lamp posts. At one point, we thought we'd lost him altogether, but it turned out he'd just bitten the top off a postbox and fallen inside.

Eventually, after sneaking past Scooby (who was lying next to a suspiciously yellow puddle) and Doo (who looked very adorable and showed absolutely no signs of the havoc he would later wreak), we managed to make it into my sitting room without waking anyone up.

I took a moment to compose myself. A LOT had happened. It's not every day you find yourself with a live gargoyle in your house. But I reminded myself that a good spy-detective never freaks out and keeps their mind on the task in hand.

'We need to be really quiet,' I whispered to Gregor and Lenny. 'My dad's an incredibly light sleeper.'

Gregor sat himself down in my dad's chair and pulled the handle which made the footrest shoot out, the back recline and Gregor shriek, 'HOLY HAGGIS BALLS!'

'*Shhhh!*' I shushed.

'What witchcraft is this?!'

'It's not witchcraft, it's just a reclining chair,' I whispered.

Gregor put his hands behind his head and let out a long sigh. '*Ahhhhhhh.* Ma bahookie has never known such luxury!'

'Your bah-whatty?' Lenny said.

'Ma backside, laddie!'

I suppose it can't be that comfortable squatting on a school roof for four hundred years.

I took the *Book of Chaos* out of my bag.

Turn my pages, read my truth, open me, OPEN ME!

'Goodness, this thing doesn't half go on,' I said.

Rich coming from you, motormouth.

'And that's quite enough from you,' I said, placing the book down on the carpet. Lenny and I sat cross-legged on either side of it, to examine it properly.

Lenny reached out a trembling hand, but I gave it a quick slap. 'Don't touch it yet!'

'But I *reaaaaaaally* like it and I'm not usually a fan of books,' he said. 'Can I lick it? It really wants me to lick it.'

'No, you cannot lick it!'

In the light, the book did look very impressive. It was bound in brown leather and seemed really old.

'I think this book might have special powers,' I said. 'Dark powers.'

Gregor rubbed his little domed tummy. 'If ye dinnae like it, I dinnae mind disposing of it for ye.'

'Gregor, I'm not going to let you eat our first proper clue. And, besides, it might be dangerous.'

Gregor shrugged. 'Fair enough.'

'Right,' I said, 'let's have a look at this thing.

My hypothesis is that, when you open it, it triggers a **SHIVER** and, when you shut it, it turns it off again. Let's see if I'm right.'

My hand hovered over the front cover, ready to flip it open.

Do it! Open me . . . Make me yours . . .

Turn my pages, turn my pages, turn my pages, TURN MY PAGES!

'This is, without doubt, the bossiest book I've ever met,' I said.

Please?

'That's better. I'm going to open it. Gregor, Lenny, are you both OK with that?'

'I mean, what's the worst that could happen? Nothing could be more horrifying than a flock of rampaging Transylvanian gargoyles,' Lenny said incorrectly.

'OK, I'm opening the book.'

'You're not, though, are you? You're just holding your hand above the book, not opening it. Shall I open the book? I want to open the book. I *really* want to open the book.'

'I'm getting ready, that's all.'

Gregor cranked the handle on the recliner and sat bolt upright.

'Look, if someone doesnae open that book, it's getting eaten.'

'Fine,' I said. 'Lenny, stop sniffing it and move out of the way. Here goes!'

CHAPTER 26
LENNY

'Hang on,' I said. 'Before we open it and unleash a **SHIVER** that could have us burping up coconuts or something, shall we see if there's any writing on the back?'

Agatha looked at me, her mouth hanging open.

'Lenny, that's actually a brilliant idea!'

It must be great to be a spy-detective assistant working for me, learning from all my great ideas.

Agatha turned the book over and we both tilted our heads.

'What's that?' she said. 'It looks like another language.'

'I can read it,' I said.

'Really?'

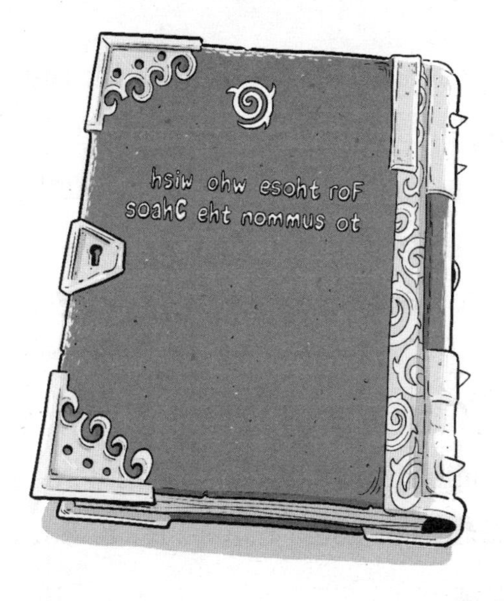

'Sure. **hsiw ohw esoht roF soahC eht nommus ot** See? Easy!'

Agatha shook her head, probably very impressed. 'I meant, do you understand it?'

'Of course not – it's another language! Want me to carry on?'

'I know it's another language, Lenny. And no, you don't have to read any more.'

'Gregor, is it Transylvanian maybe?'

'Naw, that's no' Transylvanian.'

'Maybe it's Alien,' I suggested.

Agatha looked up and said, a bit rudely, 'It's not Alien, Lenny.'

'How do you know? Do you speak Alien?'

She pulled a face that suggested she did not.

'Didn't think so, which means we can't rule it out.'

'I'm going to copy it down – just in case.' Agatha slapped my hand out of the way. 'Can you stop stroking the book, Lenny? It's both weird and distracting.'

Open me . . .

Open me!

'But I really, really want to open it.'

'Sit on your hands and try not to listen to it,' Agatha said.

'But its voice is so silky and –'

'Lenny! Hands!'

'Fine,' I said, and sat on them.

Agatha began to copy down the weird words.

kees od uoy fi egap eht nruT
,kaerw nac koob siht that soahc ehT
etihw eb kcalb dna nwod is pu erehW
.thgin si yad dna yrd era saes dnA

eb dluoc tahw dna mehyam revocsiD
.eerf srevihS eht tel uoy fI

She carried on writing for a few minutes, copying down every last letter of the gobbledegook, before putting her pen down.

'I think we're going to have to open the thing if we want to find out any more. You guys ready?'

I nodded and Gregor shrugged, then took a bite out of the TV remote, which didn't go down well with Agatha.

Once she'd wrestled it off him, she sat back down beside the book with the front cover upwards.

'I think that if we close it as soon as something strange starts happening, it will be OK. Besides, it could be that it only works at school.'

I supposed she *might* be right.

She wasn't.

Agatha pulled the book towards her. 'Yes, all right. *Book*, I'm about to open you!' and opened it.

I was secretly hoping for a monkey tail, but NOTHING happened!

'Hmmmm, that's odd . . .' Agatha said. 'No **SHIVER**.'

'You were wrong,' I said. 'It isn't the book doing it at all. Back to the drawing board. Don't feel too bad – we all make mistakes.'

I added the last bit because I'm nice, but I was worried I'd be needing a new assistant soon.

Then Gregor spluttered something, his cheeks all puffy and swollen.

'Awws issh shhoo

delishush!'

'Oh no, Agatha! Look what you've done! You've filled Gregor with coconuts! I warned you it would happen! Bad Agatha!'

Gregor swallowed. It wasn't coconuts.

'Gregor!' Agatha gasped. 'Are you eating the coffee table?'

'Och, I'm sorry. I just couldnae help ma'self!'

'You gave your word you wouldn't eat my house!'

'Aye, but the word o' a gargoyle is worth very little.'

'Stop eating things that aren't food and stop interrupting. I'm trying to figure out what to do next!'

Turn my pages . . .

Turn my pages . . .

Oi, genius, turn my pages!

The book was clearly speaking to me.

'We could turn the pages,' I suggested.

Agatha said, 'I was going to say that,' but I

think we both knew it wasn't really her day for good ideas.

On the first page there was some more Alien writing, which Agatha insisted on copying down, while the book was asking me to turn its pages and Agatha kept slapping my hand away every time I tried.

'Maybe there are some illustrations that will explain more,' she said, and finally turned a page.

I hoped so. Books are better with pictures – fact. And we were in luck because on the next page was a picture of what looked very much like a couple of kids dancing.

'Interesting, very interesting,' Agatha said, sounding quite spy-detectory, I have to admit.

'Interesting, very interesting,' I said because I wanted to sound spy-detectory too.

'Aye, really interesting,' Gregor said, not sounding interested at all because he was busy picking bits of coffee table out of his teeth with his toe talons.

But the next page was even more intriguing: there was a picture of a herd of chickens.

'Is that Margaret Hatcher?!' I shouted.

'*Shhhhh!* You'll wake everyone up!' Agatha said.

She hurriedly flicked through the following pages. The book was very big, but the pages were really thick, so there weren't that many.

'It's all there: the beards, the no gravity, the gargoyles . . .'

'Me? Is there a picture o' me?' Gregor asked, suddenly interested. 'How do I look?'

'Very gargoyle-y,' I said.

'Och good. I have been working oot,' he said, patting his belly.

'Never mind that – it's the next page I'm interested in,' Agatha said. 'What Strangeness is still to come?'

'Turn the page. Let's have a look at what we're in for,' I said very bravely.

Gregor crossed his fingers, closed his eyes and

started muttering.

'What are you doing?' Agatha said.

'Praying it's a meteor shower. I'm a wee bit peckish and I hear space rock tastes amazin'.'

'It doesn't work like that,' I told him. 'I hoped for a monkey tail and ended up losing my gravity.'

'Shall we just see?' Agatha said.

She took a deep breath and turned the page.

And a **SHIVER** pulsed through the air.

CHAPTER 27
AGATHA

'It's blank,' I said a bit flatly, because even though it was probably a good thing there wasn't a picture of a kid burping up coconuts, or a meteor shower, it felt a little anticlimactic.

'Och, wha' a let-down,' Gregor said.

I flicked through the rest of the book. There were only five pages left, and all of them were blank except the very last one, which said, in large, bold letters:

dnE ehT

'I wonder what that says?'

Lenny said, 'It says **dnE ehT**.'

I took a deep breath. 'Yes, Lenny, but what does it mean?'

Before he could answer, I felt a sudden tightness round the tops of my legs. Lenny let out a little squeak, which made me think he was feeling it too.

'Did you notice that? It must be from the **SHIVER**!' I said, the squeezing growing stronger.

I flicked back to the page after the gargoyle illustration. 'Hang on? What is *that*?'

We watched in disbelief as a drawing started to form in front of our eyes.

'Are those . . . *undercrackers*?' Gregor said.

Lenny frowned. 'They look familiar –'

He suddenly leaped to his feet, eyes bulging and a very pained look spreading across his face. 'The underpants in that picture are *my* underpants and I think they want to kill me!'

'Don't be ridiculous. There's no such thing as killer underpants!' I said, just as my own underpants betrayed me and started squeezing even tighter. I couldn't believe it – Lenny was right again!

The pressure was becoming unbearable, and I leaped up and started hopping about round Lenny.

'And this is why I dinnae believe in the things. Best to give yer bahookie some air and let it breathe,' Gregor said.

'Don't just sit there bragging about your bare bum, Gregor!' I spluttered. 'Close the book!'

Gregor hurried towards it, but before he could get there Doo suddenly bolted into the room and snatched it from the table.

'Doo! No! Bad dog,' I hissed. 'Come back here!'

Because Doo isn't the kind of dog who follows orders, he did not come back. In fact, he gave me a look that said, *Just you try and make me.*

'Go after him, Gregor,' I said, 'but don't be seen.'

Gregor hurried after Doo, saying, 'Here, doggie. Come back, doggie,' leaving Lenny and me to battle our underpants alone.

'Oh my! This is awful! They're getting tighter!'

I gasped, my eyes watering. Lenny was on his tippy-toes, desperately pulling at his waistband.

'I don't like this at all! But we need to keep quiet, or we'll wake my family.' My voice was strangled and beads of sweat were dripping down my brow.

'I'm trying!' Lenny said. Then he completed a full lap of the sitting room, fell over, and started thrashing about on the carpet, wrestling with his pants.

'Stop it, you traitors!' he groaned, his eyes crossed in agony. 'Agatha, get them *offfff*!'

I was hopping about in my own world of pain, but there was NO WAY I was going to help Lenny take off his underpants. He writhed around on the floor, trying to pull them down, and for a moment I was truly worried I was about to catch sight of his bum. But, luckily for me, it looked like his pants were fighting back. If anything, they seemed to be climbing higher up his body.

'Get them *offffffff meeeeee, pleeeeeeasssse*!' Lenny whisper-shouted again.

'No!' I whisper-shouted back, perfectly reasonably. We would get out of this situation with dignity, like professionals. Even though my own pants were climbing higher and higher and the pain was indescribable.

But then I heard a ripping sound.

'It's OK,' I said, not feeling that it was OK at all. 'They're going to tear and this will all be over! We just need to let it happen.'

Lenny whimpered.

I whimpered.

‘I don’t want to let it happen,’ Lenny said, looking at me with big, terrified eyes.

More ripping.

‘We have no choice.’ I dropped to the floor next to him and reached for his hand. ‘Be brave, Lenny. You can do this.’

Another rip.

‘Just breathe through it,’ I told him.

‘OK, breathe through it – I can do that.’ Lenny started taking very fast, shallow breaths. ‘I feel a bit dizzy.’

‘No, breathe slowly. Copy me. Breathe in . . .’

Rip!

‘Breathe out . . .’

Riiiip!

‘Breathe in . . .’

Rip!

‘Breathe out . . .’

Riiiiiiiiiiiiiiiiiiiiiiiiiiiipppppppppppppppppp!

The relief was enormous! Our bums were free!

But so were our evil underpants. And, within seconds, they were crawling their way up our bodies again, ready for a second attack.

This time on our faces.

They were trying to suffocate us!

CHAPTER 28
LENNY

I realized I had made a huge mistake that morning when I decided my pants probably had another day of wear in them. Too late I realized that my mum's warning to change my underpants more often than once a week was right. When they launched themselves at my face, I wasn't sure what was going to kill me the quickest: the smell or the tightness.

I desperately tried to pull them off, but they were clamped on fast. Although they were covering my eyes, I could tell by the noises coming from Agatha that she was in a similar situation.

'Ca . . . n't br . . . eath . . . e!' I stammered.

'Where's Gre . . . gor with that . . . booook?'

Agatha panted.

I got to my feet, still trying to yank the evil underpants off my face. I staggered around and bumped into something.

The something muffle-shouted, 'W . . . w . . . watch . . . it!' so I think it was Agatha.

I kept trying to keep the waistband away from my neck. It was exhausting and I didn't have much strength left in me.

'Can't . . . keep . . . fight . . . ing,' I stammered.

'Must . . . keep . . . fighting . . . Will not . . . be . . . beaten by my . . . own underpants,' Agatha gasped.

Just when I was beginning to see bright spots in front of my eyes, I heard the sound of yapping and scuttling talons on the carpet.

'Gregor . . . close . . . the book,' Agatha said.

'I cannae do it! This wee doggy won't let go.'

'Doo! Drop . . . it!' Agatha wheezed.

'He's no' listening to ye!' Gregor said.

'Do . . . something . . . Gregor!'

'Och, OK . . .'

There was a growl, a shout, an ***oooff,*** a ***THWUMP*** and a whimper.

And then the **SHIVER**.

My pants fell straight to the floor, and so did Agatha and I.

I breathed in great big lungfuls of sweet, sweet air.

'Thank goodness,' Agatha said when she'd caught her breath. 'Well done, Gregor!'

Gregor beamed. 'It was nowt really! A wee yappy doggie is no match for the great Gregor, son o' Scotland!'

Agatha looked around. 'Where *is* Doo? You didn't . . . eat him, did you?'

Before Gregor could answer, there was another little whimper, and we looked up to see Doo clinging to the lampshade.

'Oh, poor Doo!' Agatha said.

I didn't think 'poor Doo' at all.

I thought, *Poor Lenny.*

Doo was the one who had run off with the *Book of Chaos*, leaving me to be almost throttled to death by my own underpants.

Agatha climbed on to the half-eaten coffee table and helped Doo down. He growled at me, and then at Gregor, and trotted off with his nose in the air, like there was no need for him to apologize at all.

I slumped down on to the sofa and glared at the *Book of Chaos*. 'What are we going to do now? That book is dangerous.'

'Before I closed the book, the blank page wasnae blank any more,' Gregor said.

I blinked hard. 'What do you mean?'

'There was a picture of ye two, being attacked by yer undercrackers.'

'We have to get rid of it,' Agatha said, and gulped. 'We'll do it first thing tomorrow.'

She leaned forward and picked up the piece of paper she had copied down the cover writing on. 'I wish I could work out what this all means. And we have to find a way to make Dr Errno pay for all the trouble he's caused.'

I felt my eyes closing.

'Not now, though, Agatha. It's so late and I'm so tired and I just want to go to bed and give my bum, and my brain, some time to recover. I need some sleep before I see my dad.'

Agatha rose to her feet and picked up the book. 'You're right. I'm tired too. Let's go to bed. I'm putting this book at the bottom of my wardrobe so no one is tempted to open it, OK, Lenny?'

'Roger that!'

'Come on,' she said. 'Gregor, you can top and tail with me.'

So off we trundled to bed, with a plan to destroy the book and put an end to the Strangeness once and for all.

But we didn't count on a very unexpected visitor showing up at Agatha's first thing the following morning.

CHAPTER 29

AGATHA

I slept badly that night for three reasons:

1. I kept waking up in a cold sweat, thinking I was being strangled by my own undergarments.

2. My mind was full of questions about Dr Errno and the *Book of Chaos*. I wished I could work out what the words on the back cover meant. And I wished I knew how we were going to get rid of it. I was worried that if we destroyed the book we might unleash untold horrors. I was worried that if we kept it I might give in and open it again. It was very persistent.

3. There was a gargoyle at the bottom of my bed snoring away like a bulldozer.

Tom and George woke up early and headed downstairs to watch cartoons. Luckily, they didn't notice the gargoyle-shaped lump under my duvet and I heard them giggle about Lenny being an even louder snorer than Granny.

Lenny wasn't snoring at all, though. He actually looked very peaceful in his sleep. Almost angelic.

I kind of felt a bit fuzzy inside knowing that I actually had a friend over. In my house. Undertaking a very important mission. Even if he could be a bit of a dope sometimes.

My dad suddenly hollered up the stairs, which made me jump and woke Lenny from his slumber.

'Agatha!' Dad shouted. 'Could you come downstairs, please? And Lenny – I think you should come too.'

'Seven in the blinking morning at the weekend? Do you live in an army camp, Agatha?' Lenny said, and buried himself further down into the bottom of his sleeping bag like a grumpy caterpillar.

But there was something about the tone of my dad's voice that worried me.

'Kids!' he bellowed again.

'We'd better go and see what he wants. He's usually too busy to want to talk to me about anything.'

Lenny popped his bleary-eyed head out of the sleeping bag and said, 'But I'm *sooooooo* tired. Last night's Transylvanian gargoyle chase and super-wedgying were very traumatic and I need time to recover.'

'Agatha!' Dad shouted again. 'Don't make me come up there and get you!'

'Come on,' I said. 'We can't have him catching sight of Gregor.'

Lenny did an almighty huff and kicked himself out of his cocoon. 'Fine.'

'Gregor will be all right here for a while. We'll let him sleep.'

'Typical! Of course the *gargoyle* gets a lie-in.'

'Stop moaning! Let's see what my dad wants.'

I made sure Gregor was safely hidden and we staggered downstairs, walking a bit like cowboys because our bums were still sore.

We passed Tom and George, who had been shooed out of the house to go and play football in the back garden.

'You're in SO much trouble, Agatha,' they said together, with a little too much glee for my liking. 'There's a *teacher* here to see you.'

'Dr Errno?' That wasn't good news.

The door to the sitting room swung open and my dad said, 'At last! You two have some explaining to do.'

I gasped in surprise because standing there, arms behind his back and looking very unhappy, was Mr Pardon.

Dad had Nigel and Trevor strapped to him and was jiggling up and down in an attempt to get them to sleep, but he stared at me, right in the eyes, and said, 'Mr Pardon has come with quite a serious accusation, Agatha, and I just hope he's wrong.'

My mind was a whirl. Why was Mr Pardon here?

'I imagine you know why I'm here?' Mr Pardon said, moving his beetly eyes from Lenny to me.

I gave Lenny a look that said, *You keep quiet and leave me to do all the talking. This is a huge situation that I need to control so we don't mess it up.*

But I don't think Lenny is as good at reading looks as I am at giving them because he said, 'Is this about the Transylvanian gargoyles?'

I gave him a swift elbow in the ribs. I could not believe how quickly he'd cracked under questioning. Again.

My dad momentarily stopped jiggling, gave a splutter and said, 'This isn't a joke, Lenny.'

'I know that, Mr Topps.'

Mr Pardon's lips narrowed into a hard line. 'I believe that you have stolen something from school. Something valuable.'

That's when it all started to fall into place.

The only way Mr Pardon could know we had the book was if he'd been at the school the night before. But the mysterious figure in the corridor was Dr Errno. I was *sure* it was Dr Errno.

At least I *thought* it was Dr Errno.

Really, though, hadn't I only seen a black gown?

Actually, thinking back, the mysterious figure had perhaps been a little bit shorter than Dr Errno.

And a little bit rounder.

In fact, it had not looked at all dissimilar to Mr Pardon.

'Oh dratballs,' I said flatly, thinking back to the times we'd seen him hugging the book in the library. 'It's been you all along, hasn't it?'

'Agatha!' Dad exclaimed. 'That is no way to speak to a teacher!'

'He's not a teacher, he's a librarian,' Lenny said.

'And for that you're both very lucky, because I've come here to give you the opportunity to return what belongs to me rather than face the punishment you deserve.'

'I don't know what you're talking about,' I

said defiantly, staring at him.

There was no way I was going to give the *Book of Chaos* back to Mr Pardon. Not when I didn't know what he was planning to do with it!

'Agatha, if you've taken something belonging to Mr Pardon, you need to give it back right now, do you understand?' my dad said, trying to stick a dummy into Nigel's mouth.

I didn't want to lie, but there are sometimes things more important than telling the truth. Especially when the truth was that Mr Pardon was an evil villain trying to unleash chaos on Little Strangehaven Primary in the form of military-grade chickens and angry gargoyles. My dad would *never* believe that.

'Nope,' I said, trying to make my eyes go as big and innocent as possible, 'I haven't taken anything.'

'You were seen, Miss Topps.' Mr Pardon practically spat the words at me.

'Dad, please, you have to believe me. I can't

give it to him –'

My dad cut me off before I could finish.

'You two better get up those stairs right now and bring whatever it is you've stolen back down here, or I'll go up there and get it myself.'

I couldn't risk Dad finding Gregor, so I had no choice. We were going to have to give the book back to Mr Pardon. I'd just have to think of a way to get it back and destroy it.

'OK,' I said, through gritted teeth.

'What a shame,' Mr Pardon said. 'It must be devastating to discover your daughter is both a liar and a thief, Mr Topps.'

Dad looked at me with such disappointment that I thought I might burst into tears on the spot. I couldn't bear to think that he believed what Mr Pardon was saying.

'I did it for the right reasons, Dad, honestly . . .'

He turned his head. 'I can't even look at you right now, Agatha. This family works because we're team players. Team players don't let each other down.'

As Lenny and I trudged back to my bedroom, I tried not to think about what my dad had said, or that look in his eyes. Or how he didn't seem to know me at all. But then how could he? Just like Mum, he was always busy with everybody else but me.

Before he opened the door, Lenny turned to me and said, 'You're not a liar or a thief, Agatha. You are a very excellent spy-detective who bends the truth and looks after things that don't belong to them for the greater good. Which is essentially lying and thieving, I suppose, but it sort of feels like the right thing to do. Do you know what I mean?'

I couldn't help but smile. 'I think I do.'

'Good,' he said and opened the door. 'You can be in my team any day.'

I felt my heart swell a little. 'Lenny?' I said.

'Yup?'

'You can actually be pretty smart sometimes.'

'I know,' he said and whipped the duvet off my bed. 'Come on, Gregor. Mr Pardon wants you back.'

CHAPTER 30

LENNY

Agatha slapped her hand to her forehead.

'Oh, Lenny! He doesn't want Gregor! He wants the *Book of Chaos*!'

Oh. Really?

While my brain began processing this intriguing piece of information, Gregor – who I think I'd taken a bit by surprise – sprang out of his slumber. He jumped to his feet with his fists balled, shouting, 'I'll knock ye into the middle o' next week, ye wee feathery beasties!'

Then he noticed it was us, shook his head and said, 'Och, I'm sorry. I was having ma recurring French pigeon nightmare again. Four hundred years o' pigeons perching on yer head and pooping all over ye will do that to a gargoyle.'

Agatha took the book out from the wardrobe and said, quite snappily, 'No, I am absolutely NOT opening you now. Terrible timing, *Book of Chaos*, so please be quiet.' Then she sat down on the camp bed and said, 'I can't believe we got it so wrong!'

'Got what wrong?'

'All this time, we were so sure it was Dr Errno.'

'What was Dr Errno?'

'The person responsible for the **SHIVERS**!'

'Dr Errno isn't responsible for the **SHIVERS**?'

'No, Lenny!'

'Wow. Those hypno-nostrils are wasted on him. So who *is* responsible? Ms Stranglebum?'

'We literally just found out downstairs!'

'Your *dad* is responsible for the **SHIVERS**? Well, I did NOT see that one coming . . .'

'No, Lenny, not my dad! It's Mr Pardon!'

'Mr Pardon? But he's a *librarian*! Why would he be causing all this chaos?'

'I don't know yet, but we'll figure it out.'

'Are you really one-hundred-per-cent, bet-your-bum-on-it sure it's Mr Pardon? I just can't see it. He's all cute and squishy, with little doggies on his trousers and twinkly eyes. And he says funny things like, "Power lies in books, young man."'

Agatha screwed up her face. 'Er, he says things like *what*?'

'On my first day he said, "Power lies in books, young man." Why are you looking at me like that?'

Agatha waved the *Book of Chaos* in my face. 'Well, do you think that perhaps power *might* lie in books? *This* book, to be specific?'

'Oh. My. Goodness! Yes! Blimey, that was a clue right there! I really am an excellent spy-detective! And don't be too hard on yourself, Agatha, for not working it out. A librarian really isn't the first person you'd think of for causing chaos. He said himself that he's most orderly and organized. But you know what?'

'What?' Agatha said a little wearily.

'I kind of think: good for Mr Pardon. Breaking down stereotypes. Showing that librarians have it in them to be evil baddies too.'

'Seriously, Lenny?'

'What?'

'Just stop talking. I need to work out what to do. Mr Pardon is downstairs, waiting for the book.'

'We could just tear it up now?' I suggested.

She shook her head. 'I think destroying it is too dangerous. Who knows what could happen? We might accidentally start a wave of **SHIVERS** we can't stop! We need to figure out more about how the book works first.'

'Well, why *don't* we give him Gregor instead?'

'Oi! Ye traitor!'

'I'm just throwing ideas out there. Don't take it personally, buddy!'

'We're not giving him Gregor,' Agatha said.

'We could substitute it for another book?' I walked over to her bedside table and held up a large hardback. '*Ninety-nine Ways to Neutralize an Enemy - Volume Seven*? Near enough?'

Agatha closed her eyes and drew a deep, deep breath.

That girl must have big lungs because it took a while.

'Something tells me he might spot the difference,' she eventually said. 'For a start, the spy-detetective manual doesn't talk, does it?'

Before we were able to improve on my frankly quite brilliant book-swap idea, the door swung open and Agatha's dad burst in.

'What is taking so long –'

He stopped in his tracks. 'WHAT IN THE NAME OF ALL THINGS HOLY,' he shouted, pointing at Gregor, 'IS *THAT*?'

Gregor froze.

'It's a . . .' stammered Agatha. 'It's a . . . model. We made it at school.'

Agatha's dad peered at Gregor suspiciously. 'It looks so lifelike,' he said. 'Almost real.'

I could see Gregor was holding his breath, trying not to move. Mr Topps prodded Gregor in the belly button. 'Did you not think of putting some clothes on it, though?'

He walked behind Gregor and peered even closer. 'And what's that growing out of the small fella's backside?'

'Mr Topps!' Mr Pardon shouted from downstairs. 'I really must be going. I do have other things to occupy my weekend.'

'Yes, of course. Sorry, I was just . . .' He looked at Gregor again. 'Never mind. We'll be right down.'

He held out his hand. 'Agatha, give the book to me, please.'

Agatha hesitated, then passed it over.

'The *Book of Chaos*? Sounds like it could be about this place.'

He began to open the cover, but Agatha shouted, 'Dad, don't!' and luckily he shut it again before he started turning pages and set off a **SHIVER**.

'Look, Dad, I really don't think it's a good idea for you to give that to Mr Pardon. We've been investigating him and we think the book might be . . . evil.'

'Oh, *I'm* not going to give it to him, young lady,' he said, handing it back. 'You are. I'll see you downstairs.'

And he left.

As soon as he had gone, Gregor let out a huge breath and collapsed on the floor.

'I thought I was done for!' he exclaimed, panting. 'But what did he mean about something growing out o' ma bahookie?'

'You've got a bit of a moss situation back there,' I said.

While Gregor turned in circles, trying to inspect his own bum, Agatha and I headed downstairs to face the music.

Reluctantly, Agatha handed the *Book of Chaos* to Mr Pardon. He clutched it close to his chest as if it was a newborn baby, then gave it a long, deep sniff. 'You're back where you belong now, my bookums-snookums.' Clutching it closer, he whispered into its spine, 'Monday, yes, I promise I'll do it on Monday.'

Agatha's dad gave a slight frown, then said, 'Agatha, Lenny, do you have something you want to say to Mr Pardon? Clearly, this book is very important to him and it's always best to make peace with people you've wronged.'

'Nope, not really,' Agatha said.

'Agatha! Apologize this instant!'

Agatha stared so hard at Mr Pardon I wondered if she might be trying to burn him with her eyes. Finally, she said, 'I'm sorry, Mr Pardon,' in a tone that did not sound at all sorry.

And I said, 'Yeah, I'm sorry,' in a tone that was equally unsorry.

'I'm sorry too,' Agatha's dad then added, in a tone that, in all fairness, did actually sound quite sorry. 'I don't know what's got into them.'

Mr Pardon sniffed. 'No matter. I have what I came for,' and scuttled off.

Agatha's dad turned to me. 'And I'm afraid I'm going to have to call your mother to let her know about this.'

'Oh, mouldy matzo balls, Mr Topps! Really?'

'Yes, Lenny, really.'

CHAPTER 31
AGATHA

When we got back to my room, Gregor was examining his bum with my hand mirror.

'Aye, that's a bad case o' Creeping Crevice Moss, and no mistake,' he said. 'I'll be needing some extra-strength weedkiller on that.'

'Could we move on to more pressing issues?' I suggested. 'Mr Pardon has the *Book of Chaos* and we have to get it back before something *really* bad happens.'

'Ye've clearly never had a case o' Creeping Crevice Moss,' Gregor mumbled.

'Monday,' Lenny said, completely out of nowhere.

'Monday?'

'That's what Mr Pardon whispered to the book: "I promise I'll do it on Monday."'

'Why Monday?' I said.

'Well, Mum says it's good to get all your big jobs done at the start of the week.'

'Possibly,' I said, not thinking that was the reason at all. 'At least he's not going to do anything before then.'

I cleared a space on the floor, took out the piece of paper that I'd used to copy the words from the *Book of Chaos*, and held it out so we all could see.

'Look, we don't have long before Lenny's mum will be here to pick him up. We have to figure out what this says. Everybody concentrate.'

We all leaned in and looked at the first line:

!soahc eht nommus ot hsiw ohw esoht roF

'Any ideas?' I asked hopefully.

It looked like gobbledegook to me and if *I* couldn't figure it out I had a suspicion nobody else would.

But then Lenny said, 'Oooh, I know!' And I did get my hopes up a little, until he followed this up with, 'Pretty sure that's Alien.'

And then Gregor said, 'It looks like an ancient, murky forest to me,' and reached over to inspect his backside with the mirror again.

I was about to tell them both to focus when something caught my eye.

'Quick, Gregor! Give that here!'

Gregor looked a bit confused and then handed me a small clump of moss, which I quickly dropped.

'Gah! No! I meant the mirror!' I said, wiping

my hand on my pyjamas.

He passed the mirror over and I held it up to the paper. 'Look – the letters are backwards!'

'Whoa,' Lenny said. 'I really had my money on it being Alien.'

I read the first line:

For those who wish to summon the chaos!

Before I could get any further, Lenny interrupted me with a '*Dun-dun-duuuuunnnnnn!*'

'Lenny, I don't think you're taking this seriously.'

'Sorry, got carried away. It won't happen again.'

I cleared my throat and continued.

Turn the page if you do seek
The chaos that this book can wreak,
Where up is down and black be white
And seas are dry and day is night.

Discover mayhem and what could be
If you let the Shivers free.
Through the portal, crossing space,
Where rules and order have no place.

Read the pages one by one
Until the world you know is gone,
Stolen through the gateway door,
Order lost, your world – no more.

'Right, well' I said, not quite sure what to say after that.

'And this is why I don't read books!' Lenny said. 'I did not enjoy that AT ALL! Who wants to read about their world being destroyed? Not me, that's for sure.'

'It isn't the most positive thing I've ever read, but let's think about what we've learned, shall we?' I said, trying not to be too much of a misery guts.

'Och, it seems pretty simple to me. It sounds like if ye finish the book then the world ends,'

Gregor said very matter-of-factly.

'And, if every time someone turns to a blank page it gets filled in – like it did with that underpants picture – how many pages are still blank?' Lenny asked.

I tried to sound very not-panicky, but my voice came out a bit more wibbly-wobbly than I would have liked. 'I think I counted five. But we filled one with the underpants attack. So four, and if those last pages are filled and four more **SHIVERS** are released, the world as we know it, or Little Strangehaven Primary at least, could be destroyed.'

'So, if Mr Pardon fills in the last page, then it's THE END?!' Lenny said.

'That's what the poem suggests.'

'Like the *end* end?'

'Yup, the *end* end.'

'Well, isn't this a cheery conversation for a Saturday morning?' Gregor said.

'I don't understand!' Lenny wailed. 'Why does Mr Pardon want an *end* end?'

'I don't know why he wants an *end* end! What makes a bad guy want anything?'

'Oooh, I know!' Lenny said, sounding surprisingly excited under the circumstances. 'He might have accidentally been exposed to gamma rays –'

'Lenny, he's not the Incredible Hulk.'

'OK . . . How about . . . he became the host for an alien with an amorphous, liquid-like form?'

I took a breath and reminded myself not to lose patience. 'Like Venom, from Spider-Man?'

'Exactly!'

'No, Lenny.'

'Or maybe he fell into a vat of chemical waste –'

'Don't think he has anything in common with the Joker either.'

'OK, well, I'm sure he'll tell us at the end, in the part where we confront him for his evil deeds. The bad guys always spill when they have their moment in the spotlight.'

'I'm sure he will,' I said, 'but I can't help

thinking it might be a little too late by then.'

'I hope he has a really good reason. I worry that it's going to be something boring because he's a librarian,' Lenny continued.

'Shall we leave that for the time being? What we really need to worry about is getting that book back before we reach the *end* end.'

'And wha' do we do wi' it when we get it back, lassie?' Gregor said. 'No offence, but I'm no' sure you two should be left in charge o' something that's a gateway to a world o' chaos. In fact, ye'd be the absolute last people I'd be leaving wi' something so important.'

'I find that a little offensive, Gregor. But you may have a point. There's a bit more writing left. Maybe it will tell us how to dispose of the book safely. Shall I read on?'

'There's MORE?' Lenny shouted. 'I'm not sure I want to know any more.'

'Terrible attitude, Lenny,' I said, and carried on anyway.

To those who sense the SHIVERS come,
Listen up, my special ones.

'That's the best bit so far. I don't mind being called special,' Lenny interrupted. 'Does it mention anything about our specialness being linked to extra mole belly buttons?'

'No, it does not! Now hush!'

When they forget and you do not,
They will believe you've lost the plot.
But chaos lives inside of you –
Search yourself: you'll see it's true.

Thus only you can stop The End,
But don't destroy what's out on lend,
For if this book does cease to be
Oblivion awaits both you and me.

'Oh well, that's a relief,' Lenny said.

'What do you mean?' Gregor and I looked at

each other in confusion.

'We just need to destroy the book and everything will be A-OK!'

'In what world is oblivion *A-OK*?' I asked.

'Because, if I remember correctly, oblivion is the place where all your wishes are granted! You know, where you can ride giant frogs and Mr Whippy ice cream comes out of your taps and your mum and dad still live together? Or – at the very least – your tiny shampoos outnumber your Pez dispensers. It's . . . a bit like heaven?'

Gregor and I said nothing.

'By the look on your faces, I'm thinking I might not have the meaning of oblivion completely correct?'

'No, Lenny. That's not what oblivion means.'

I didn't comment on Lenny's version of heaven because who was I to judge? But I'd definitely rather have a James Bond gadget-car to take me places, and magic laundry that washed itself, and live in a place where babies didn't cry all night and could look after themselves.

Gregor stepped in with a detailed explanation. 'Oblivion means complete annihilation, total termination, nothing but nothingness, everybody goes bye-bye –'

'You mean . . . the *end* end?' Lenny said, his eyes wide and jaw on the floor. 'Again?'

I put my hand on his shoulder. 'Yes, Lenny, the *end* end. Again.'

'This book is rubbish. I give it NO stars.'

'What do you think it means when it says, *Chaos lives inside of you*?' I asked.

'No idea,' Lenny said.

'I might *live* in chaos, but I don't think chaos is inside me too. Is it?' I said, not really liking that thought.

A shout came up the stairs.

'Lennox Tuchus! Get down here now! You have some serious explaining to do! You do realize you're grounded for all eternity?'

Lenny turned a little grey. 'Oh matzo balls!

That's my mum! The oblivion has started . . .'

He grabbed his things. Then he paused and said, 'Saturday . . .'

And I said, 'Yeah, it's Saturday. You OK?'

He gave himself a shake. 'It's nothing. Just thought my dad might come and get me, that's all.'

'Maybe he got caught up with his work again?' I said.

'Yeah, maybe,' Lenny said, but he didn't sound convinced.

'We need to meet extra early at school on Monday,' I said, changing the subject. 'At seven o'clock, we need to be ready to take down Mr Pardon before he starts flicking through the pages.'

Lenny nodded and dashed out of the room.

I looked over at Gregor, who was gnawing the leg of my chair. I had a lot of planning to do, but for the time being I mainly needed to focus on keeping a gargoyle hidden from the rest of my family and stopping him from eating our house.

CHAPTER 32
LENNY

I spent the rest of the weekend trying to convince my mum that I was not on 'a quick road to ruin', whatever that meant, that she hadn't failed as a parent, and that Agatha was not going to grow up to be a criminal mastermind. Although I wasn't one hundred per cent certain about that last one.

I also spent a long time thinking about Mr Pardon and how he could have become an evil villain. My main theory centred round poisonous ink fumes from the library books messing with his brain lobes.

I thought a bit about my dad as well and tried not to feel too sad. He'd be doing something really important. Probably.

On Monday morning I arrived at school bang on time. Agatha was already there, her bag at her feet and her arms crossed, looking at me furiously.

'WHERE HAVE YOU BEEN?' she blared at me. 'WE'VE BEEN WAITING FOR AN HOUR! I SAID SEVEN O'CLOCK!'

Turns out listening carefully is not my area of expertise. But who needs to listen carefully to be a spy-detective? Exactly. Nobody. I once heard that Sherlock Holmes never listened carefully to anything, ever. I think it was Sherlock Holmes . . . I wasn't listening carefully at the time.

'Poor Gregor has been stuck in my backpack all this time,' Agatha said, still eyeballing me.

A muffled but definitely irritated voice said, 'Mornin', Lenny. Nice of ye to show up *finally*.'

'You brought him to school?'

'I could hardly leave him at home, could I?!'

'Are you OK? You seem a bit tense.'

'I am tense, Lenny. It's been a rather stressful weekend. Gregor ate all our neighbour's garden gnomes, my parents are still furious with me and there's a very good chance that Mr Pardon of all people is going to destroy Little Strangehaven Primary. He only has to open the *Book of Chaos* four more times and that's it – the end of everything. And, if you must know, I also stepped on a snail

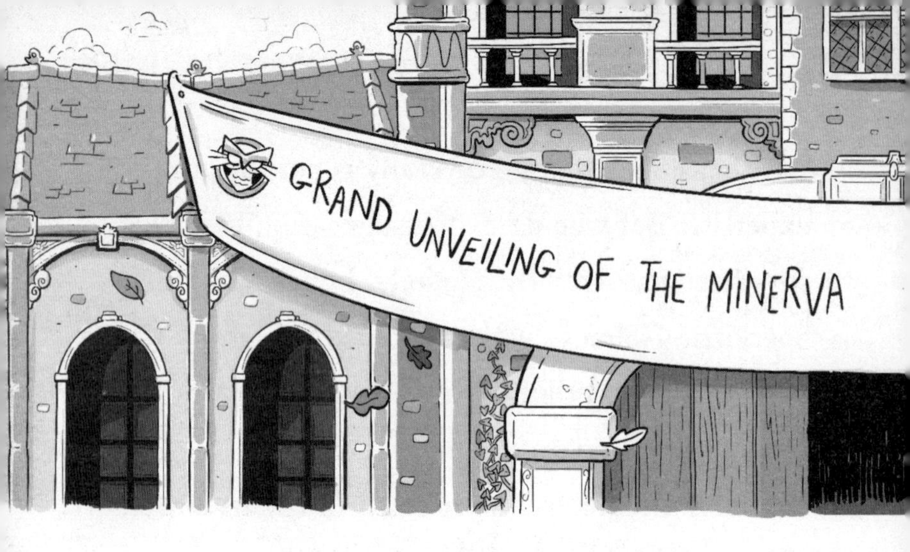

on the way here and I'm feeling very guilty about it, OK?!'

I wasn't sure which one of those issues was bothering her most, so I just picked one and hoped for the best.

'Would you like to talk about the garden gnomes?' I asked kindly.

'No, Lenny, I do not want to talk about the massacre that occurred in Mr Fenwick's garden.'

'It wasnae ma fault! Their jolly wee faces just said *eat me*. It was impossible to resist,' Gregor called out.

'I DO NOT want to discuss it,' Agatha snapped.

I tried again. 'The snail then? I shouldn't worry about it. I once accidentally ate three woodlouses –'

'How do you accidentally eat *three* woodlice? One, I could – Actually, forget it. I don't want to know. We have more important things to worry about.'

She pointed at a banner hanging over the huge mahogany doors, where Gregor used to sit.

'*Grand unveiling of the Minerva Automated Librarian System*,' I read out.

'That has to be something to do with why Mr Pardon is going to finish the *Book of Chaos* today.

We need to find it before he unleashes some terrible Strangeness from its pages. Now come on – we've got just under an hour before registration.'

I stuck out my elbow – I knew she was about to drag me by it, so I didn't see any point in putting up a fight.

'Where are we going?'

'To the library.'

'And why are we going to the library?' I said, almost too scared to ask.

'To get the book back OBVIOUSLY!'

'I don't think Mr Pardon's going to let us borrow it,' I said, which I think was a reasonable statement. 'He sounded properly annoyed on Saturday.'

'We're not going to borrow it; we're going to steal it, *duh*!'

I did not appreciate that 'duh', so I said, 'What if we can't find it? What then? It might not even be at school!' And then I added my own '*duh*', which felt pretty good.

'Mr Pardon will be at school. Do librarians even exist if they're outside libraries?' Agatha continued. 'And, if he's in school, the *Book of Chaos* has to be *in the school.* And we will not stop until we find it, OK?'

Not stop? That needed some clarification.

'What if I get hungry? Can I stop then?'

'No.'

'What if I need a drink?'

'No.'

'What if I'm busting for the loo?'

'Yes, all right, you can stop for a wee if it's *absolutely* necessary.'

'OK, I can handle those terms! Let's find this book!'

CHAPTER 33
AGATHA

We made our way to the library, doing some pretty impressive spy-slinking down the corridor. At least *I* was slinking. Lenny still had a bit of his squid thing going on. It was becoming somewhat of a strain carrying my bag, though. Gregor was pretty heavy.

Lenny must have noticed I was struggling because he said, 'Agatha, allow me. I'm known for my upper-body strength.'

'Known where? In the world of teddy-bear wrestling?'

'Do you want me to carry it or not?' he shot back.

I did want him to carry it, so I handed it over.

Anyway, halfway to the library, we were stopped in our tracks by the sound of a commotion. We bundled into the nearest classroom and I strained to make out what was going on, but it was tricky over Gregor's ear-shattering snoring. His weekend of gnome-savaging had obviously worn him out. I screwed my eyes shut so I could concentrate on the sound of raised voices in the corridor.

'Agatha,' Lenny said, 'do you need a poo? Because now is not a good time.'

I opened my eyes. 'No, Lenny. I do not need a poo. Now shush and listen!'

'Mr Pardon, I'm afraid your refusal to work alongside Minerva really left me no choice. I made it quite clear on Friday that your job would change but now I'm afraid to say that your employment at Little Strangehaven Primary has been terminated.'

'I understand, Dr Errno. I'll just collect a few personal items and then I'll leave.'

'Well, good. Look, you were due to retire in a

few years anyway. Why not see this as an opportunity?'

'An opportunity? I suppose it is, in a way,' Mr Pardon said, and laughed like a true evil villain.

I gasped, then whispered to Lenny to make sure he was up to speed, 'Mr Pardon has been terminated.'

Lenny's face lit up. 'Oh, well that was easy. Rest in peace, Mr Pardon. Shall we go and hang out in the playground?'

'No, Lenny, he's been given the axe.'

'The axe? Why?! That's a terrible idea. Now he's got a terrifying book *and* something to chop us up with.'

'Lenny, Mr Pardon has been fired!'

'Fired? Out of what? A cannon?'

'LENNOX! Mr Pardon has lost his job!'

'Did he check where he last had it?'

'Lenny, please can you focus? Mr Pardon is no longer allowed to be a librarian at this school.'

Lenny paled. 'He's not going to like that! He's

definitely going to want to start flicking through that book of his now!'

'Exactly!'

We heard footsteps coming towards us and ducked down so we couldn't be spotted. Through the window in the classroom door, I could just see Dr Errno marching down the corridor.

Mr Pardon shouted after him, 'You will live to regret this, Reginald! Mark my words. I will destroy you and your school!'

'You have an hour to leave the building, Henry. I want you off the premises before Ms Stranglebum arrives to unveil our new robot librarians!' Dr Errno called over his shoulder. 'I'm very sad it has come to this, but Pamela Stranglebum is my future! I mean, the future of the school!'

'There's a reign of chaos over this school!' Mr Pardon hollered back. 'Soon you will learn what happens when you don't have a Custodian of Order to protect you!'

There was some angry stomping, then silence,

and I turned to Lenny to discuss our next move.

'First things first,' he said, rolling up his sleeves. 'Let's get that axe off Mr Pardon.'

'There is no axe! It's the *Book of Chaos* we need!'

'Yeah, and that! To the library!'

Quickly, we slunk along the corridor. Lenny was moving very fast, which made me realize something.

'Er, Lenny, where's my bag?'

He immediately stopped, a guilty expression filling his face. 'Oooh, I do not know.'

'Lenny! You said you'd carry it!'

'I did . . . for a bit, but it was very heavy!'

'What about your upper-body strength? Gah! Gregor was in there! Where did you put it?'

'I *may* have left him in the classroom.'

So back to the classroom we slunk.

'It's not here! Lenny, you just can't leave bags containing sleeping gargoyles lying around!'

'Don't panic! There it is!'

'Where?'

'Right there!' Lenny said, pointing at Jordan, who was walking down the corridor with a sleeping gargoyle unknowingly strapped to his back.

'Oh dratballs! Jordan's stealing my bag!' I fumed. 'This is all we need!'

Mr Pardon would have to wait. Right then, we had to get Gregor back – a spy-detective never leaves a team member behind.

I raced after Jordan, only just stopping before I bowled into him. 'Jordan,' I panted, 'that's my bag.'

'I know. No one else would be caught dead with this tatty old thing,' he said and slung it on to the floor with a **THWUMP**. 'What have you got in here, bricks?'

He bent over like he might be about to open it up.

Lenny and I both shouted, 'No!' at the same time.

'Oh, Little Puke, I didn't see you there, what with you being so little.' Jordan smiled an evil smile. 'What *have* you got in here that you don't want me to see so badly?'

'Nothing. Just books,' I said as casually as I could.

'Really heavy books,' Lenny added. 'Books with loads more words than regular books. It's all the extra words that make them heavier, see?'

I didn't see, so I doubted Jordan would.

'Why are you here so early anyway? You shouldn't be in the building yet,' Jordan said.

'Why are *you* here so early?' I shot back.

'My dad works here, stupid. I'm always early.'

'We're here for early-morning library club,' I said.

Jordan squinted, like he was sizing us up. Eventually, he said, 'Nah, don't believe you.' And he bent down and started to pull the zip on my bag.

'I *really* wouldn't do that if I was you,' I said.

'Do what? This?' Jordan said, and he opened the bag.

Gregor leaped out, bopped him right on the

nose, and shouted, 'Take that, ye great feathery beastie!'

Jordan stood there for a moment, in complete shock, his eyes rattling around in his head and his mouth open, before finally toppling backwards.

I bent down and shook his shoulders. 'Did you knock him out?'

'In ma defence, I was in the middle of ma pigeon nightmare when he woke me,' Gregor said, scratching his bum-moss.

Like the professional I am, I reacted quickly to the unfolding situation. 'We need to get him out of here before someone sees.' I took hold of Jordan's leg and started dragging him. 'Don't just stand there like statues – give me a hand!'

'To be fair, I am a statue,' Gregor said.

'Statues don't dream about pigeon fights. Now grab a leg and pull!'

Lenny did as instructed and grabbed Jordan's other leg. Gregor, however, sat on top of his belly for a ride, which wasn't helpful by any stretch of the imagination. But somehow we managed to bundle Jordan into the cupboard where Cleaner

Wiener stored all his mops, brooms, loo rolls and paper towels.

'Do you think he'll be OK?' Lenny asked.

'I'm sure his dad will find him later,' I said.

I held open my bag. 'Right, Gregor, climb back in. We're off to get the *Book of Chaos* from Mr Pardon before he's tempted to turn those final pages and bring about oblivion.'

'Och, do I have to? I cannae be any use stuck in a sack!'

I gave him my best *don't mess with me* eyes, which were highly effective as usual, and he clambered in.

'Lenny, you can carry him, but you absolutely have to promise not to leave him anywhere this time.'

'Totally promise,' Lenny lied.

'Right, let's go!'

CHAPTER 34
LENNY

I was completely up for going straight to the library to confront Mr Pardon and prise the book from his hands, but the thought of the doom that awaited should we not succeed caused something to stir within me.

When I told Agatha, she wasn't very pleased. Which seemed unfair.

'Don't look at me like that!' I said.

Agatha crossed her arms and huffed. 'You really can't wait?'

'No, Agatha. I can't wait. I can feel it. It's on its way to the departure lounge. Besides, we agreed it in the terms.'

'Good spy-detectives can tune out any calls of

nature during periods of high action and imminent danger. Are you a good spy-detective, Lenny?'

Rude question from an assistant, but I said, '*Obviously*, Agatha.'

'Good, then let's go.'

My stomach did a big cramp, like it was not happy with that suggestion, and I bent over and groaned. 'Nope, not happening, I'm afraid.'

'Fine!' she said, throwing her arms in the air. 'Go to the toilet then!'

'Thank you, I will.'

She pointed an angry finger at me. 'And nothing better happen while I'm waiting!'

'It totally won't! Relax!'

I find it very annoying when Agatha's right and I'm wrong. As it turned out, this was one of those *reaaallly* rare times and, on reflection, we probably shouldn't have relaxed. Because something DID happen.

And it happened when I was sitting on the toilet.

I'd waltzed into the cloakroom, and bumped straight into a gang of big Year Six boys. The morning prefects. They had a reputation for being super tough on the younger kids.

'Lower-school toilets are at the other end of the corridor,' the biggest one said.

'Need . . . to . . . go . . . now,' I said and, deciding it was the lesser of two evils, shoved past them.

'I'm writing your name down in the *Prefects' Book of Wrongdoings*!' one of them called out.

I wasn't worried about that. I had bigger issues . . .

I whipped my trousers down and sat on the loo just in time, with a massive sigh of relief and a real feeling of triumph.

It was only once I'd finished my business that I noticed there was no toilet roll.

I closed my eyes. This really was not ideal, mid-mission. But there was nothing for it. I had to believe that the prefects' sense of decency and fair

play would win through when they recognized a fellow man in trouble.

'Psst! Hey! Can somebody chuck me some loo roll? There's none in here!'

Let me say that the prefects were *not* sympathetic. On the contrary, they burst out laughing – which was not very prefectly – and I sat there, blushing.

That wasn't even the *something* that happened,

though. That *something* happened next.

While I was trapped in the loo, pondering my next step, I felt the **SHIVER**. The strange rippling that could only mean one thing: Mr Pardon had opened the *Book of Chaos*.

Terrible timing, Mr Pardon.

My super-spy-detective instincts told me I had to get back to Agatha, fast.

I won't tell you exactly what I had to do then, but let's just say I left the bathroom with one sock fewer than I went in with.

As I pulled up my trousers, a strange groaning noise echoed round the bathroom.

I presumed – incorrectly – that it must be one of the prefects having a bit of a struggle on the loo. I sympathized, but what was I supposed to do? I unlocked my stall door, and walked out.

The Year Sixes were not there.

Well, they were, but they weren't themselves. Far, far from it.

They were wrapped from head to foot in toilet

roll, with two tiny slits where their eyes were. The *Book of Chaos* had struck again and had turned them all into mummies.

Toilet-paper mummies.

They turned as one, arms outstretched, and started walking towards me.

I was pretty certain they didn't want to hug me. In fact, I was more leaning towards them wanting to kill me, on account of them groaning, '*Killlll . . . hiiiim . . . KILL . . . HIMMMM . . .*'

Year Six mummy boys are way meaner than regular Year Six boys. And there was no escape – they were blocking the door.

So I did the only thing a brave spy-detective could do – I screamed for my assistant to help.

But Agatha didn't come.

The mummies continued to stagger towards me, their toilet-paper-draped hands reaching for my neck.

I had to think fast. Well, at least faster than they were moving towards me. Which actually

wasn't that speedy, so really I had quite a bit of time.

Luckily, I had a brainwave. I knew I could depend on my trusty brain, unlike my untrusty assistant. I ducked past one of the mummies and made it to the sink. I turned a tap on at full blast, stuck my finger in the spout and directed the jet of water straight at them.

'Ha! Take that, Year Six mummy boys!'

The water splashed their toilet-paper bandages, which they did not like ONE LITTLE BIT.

They shuffled back, trying to protect their wrappings from getting more of a soaking.

I angled the jet of water at them again, and again they shuffled out of the line of fire and further away from the door.

I shoved past them and ran out into the corridor. I was free!

But there, in front of me, was another toilet-paper mummy.

But this wasn't any ordinary mummy. I'd

recognize those eyes anywhere. This was an Agatha-mummy. And she raised her arms and started staggering towards me.

‘*Kiiiillll . . . Lennnoxxxx . . .*’

‘No, Agatha! Don’t kill me! Naughty assistant!’

I began tearing at the toilet paper as she clasped me round the throat. She squeezed and I could hardly breathe.

‘*Nooo!*’

I scrabbled at her wrappings, pulled them, yanked them, and finally they fell completely away from her head. Suddenly she seemed to wake from her trance, and then her eyes filled with confusion.

‘Wha . . . what’s going on?’

‘*Letttt . . . gooo oh my froaaatt!*’ I rasped.

Agatha immediately released me, and looked at her hands, baffled.

‘It was the *Book of Chaos*!’ I said, rubbing my neck. ‘Mr Pardon must have opened it again, and everybody turned into toilet-paper mummies!’

‘But why didn’t *you*?’ she asked.

I shrugged. 'Maybe because there was none in my stall? Hang on . . . Why were you in the loo? Did you go for a wee too? What happened to your powerful spy-detective bladder?'

Before Agatha could answer, the door to the stock cupboard burst open.

'Look,' I said, pointing, 'mummy-Jordan!'

Mummy-Jordan started to stagger towards us, joining up with the Year Six mummy boys who had found their way out of the toilet.

'We've no time to lose! New plan: we find Mr Pardon and get that book. Let's go, trusty assistant!' I said, my excellent brain thinking at warp speed.

'Let's go, trusty WHAT did you say?' Agatha snapped, looking more like she wanted to kill me then than she had done when she was a mummy.

'Just trying it out,' I said. '"Assistant Agatha" has a good ring to it, don't you think?'

She glared at me, and opened her mouth, but before she could say anything we felt it again.

The **SHIVER**!

All the mummy kids stopped in their very slow tracks. They began pulling their loo-roll bandages off and slowly came to their senses.

'Thank goodness for that,' I said.

'Don't relax just yet. Mr Pardon could turn another page at any moment. He's a librarian on the edge, Lenny. We need to find him! There's only three pages left now!'

'OK, follow me,' I said.

'Er, Lenny . . .'

'Not now, Agatha. I'm leading the mission. I'm Leader Lenny!'

'LENNOX!'

'WHAT IS IT, ASSISTANT AGATHA?'

'Where's my bag?'

CHAPTER 35

AGATHA

So now, in a relatively short space of time, we had managed to lose Gregor *twice*.

When I say *we*, I really mean Lenny.

It was time to take charge. Again.

'As I see it, this mission now has four objectives. They are as follows:

'One: locate Mr Pardon and retrieve the *Book of Chaos* before he destroys the school.

'Two: find Gregor before he eats the school. He's always hungry after he wakes up.

'Three: hide the *Book of Chaos* in a place where no one can ever find it.

'Four: turn Mr Pardon in to the Library Authorities. If there even is such a thing.'

'Sounds good to me. You know what, Agatha? If I was paying you to be my assistant, I'd give you a raise.'

'Thank you. What? No! I'm not your assistant. Argh! You're so annoying. Anyway, we have to achieve all four objectives before Mr Pardon turns those last three pages and Little Strangehaven Primary is destroyed!'

'*Dun-dun-dunnnnnn!*' Lenny said as I grabbed him by the elbow and charged off down the corridor.

'Where are we going?' Lenny asked when he'd finished his dramatics.

'To the library.' I pointed to a big hole in the wall. 'And, by the looks of those bite marks, I think Gregor might have headed that way too. I bet he's on an eating rampage again. I should have let him eat *two* paving slabs this morning.'

It was getting close to morning registration and kids had started filing in from the playground, forcing us to weave in and out of them.

Lenny shouted helpful things like, 'Get out of the way, fellow students! Little Strangehaven Primary is headed for oblivion! Which is *not* a good thing, in case you're wondering!'

But nobody took any notice. Nobody ever takes any notice of Year Fours.

Nobody paid any attention to the next **SHIVER** either.

'That's only two pages left until total annihilation,' Lenny said, which did nothing for my stress levels.

We carried on through the corridors, waiting for the next terrible thing to happen, but, despite the *Book of Chaos* having been opened, I felt completely normal.

Which was unnerving.

I put the feeling of impending doom to one side and carried on towards the library. There was another banner over the door announcing the unveiling of the Minerva robots, but this one looked liked someone – probably Mr Pardon – had ripped it in half.

I said, 'Right, get your spy-detective head on and follow my lead – we're going in.'

I turned to smile encouragingly, but Lenny was nowhere to be seen.

I looked up and down, and this way and that, but there was absolutely no trace of him.

Had he run out on me mid-mission? It was possible, I supposed. Probable, in fact. Not everyone is as professional as I am.

But then I heard someone who sounded a lot like Lenny say, 'Agatha, where are you?' There was a pause, followed by, 'Useless assistant . . .'

'Lenny?'

'Ah, Agatha. I didn't see you there or I wouldn't have mentioned how useless you are. Actually . . . I still don't see you. Where are you?'

That's when I figured out what Strangeness the *Book of Chaos* had brought this time.

'Aha! I know what's happened,' I said.

'You do?'

'Yes! Don't you see?'

'Not you, I don't!'

'And that's because I'm invisible. And you are too!'

'I'm not invisible! I can hear myself talking.'

'Hold up your hand, Lenny. Can you see it?'

I heard a little yelp. 'Nope. Did it fall off?'

'No! It's still there, just invisible.'

'Are you sure?'

'Yes. Slap your face if you don't believe me.'

There was the sound of a slap, closely followed by an 'ow'. 'Agatha! What did you tell me to do that for?'

'You could have clapped, I suppose,' I said, smiling because he couldn't see me. 'Now, Lenny, this is an extreme situation and I don't want you to panic –'

'Panic? Why would I panic? Think what I can do with this power! I could rob banks! Break into sweet shops! Sneak into a zoo at night and cuddle some meerkats!'

'Do you want to do all that now, or would you prefer to use our sudden invisibility to help us creep up on Mr Pardon, save Gregor, and us, and also the rest of Little Strangehaven Primary from eternal doom?'

'Those things too, I suppose,' he said a bit half-heartedly.

'Then let's sneak into the library now before

he closes the book again.'

Lenny tried the door handle. 'Matzo balls! It's locked! But don't worry,' he said, immediately causing me to worry. 'I have an idea.'

'Wait, Lenny –' I started.

But it was too late. He'd already put his idea into action.

CHAPTER 36
LENNY

My trusty super-brain came to the rescue again. Well done, super-brain!

Since I was invisible, I could just run through the library door!

I backed away a few paces, so I could get a good run-up, took a deep breath and started sprinting as fast as I could.

And then I **SMASHED** head first into the door.

I lay on the floor, staring at the ceiling, my head throbbing.

'What was that bang?' Agatha said from somewhere close by. 'It sounded like someone running into a door!'

I didn't say anything.

'Lenny . . . did you get confused and think that because you're invisible you can walk through doors?'

'No,' I lied.

'Lenny?' said Agatha. 'Are you lying on the floor?'

'No,' I said, jumping up.

And then I watched as the door handle turned and the door opened. I gasped.

'What *is* it with you and doors?' Agatha said.

'Clearly, the *Book of Chaos* must have made the lock act strangely,' I said.

'Possibly. Or maybe the door wasn't locked and needed to be pushed not pulled?'

'Who can say?' I said. 'I guess we'll never know. Now follow me – I'm going in.'

'Actually, I think *you* should follow *me*,' Agatha said.

We must have both stepped forward at the same time because we managed to get ourselves wedged in the doorway, which Agatha blamed me for, but was clearly her fault.

After a bit of a tussle, we got into the library and I began spy-slinking around for clues. Which, thinking about it now, wasn't necessary because I was invisible.

There was a strange noise, a huffing, puffing, strained sort of groaning, but I couldn't figure out where it was coming from.

I scanned the room for any sign of Gregor or Mr Pardon or the *Book of Chaos*.

Bookshelves, table, chair, light, fire extinguisher, bin, door to a secret room, bookcase, robot owls in their docking stations, desk –

Hang on . . . REWIND!

Door to a secret room?!

'Agatha, do you see that secret room?' I said.

'The one that has a sign over the door saying ROOM OF DANGEROUS AND FORBIDDEN BOOKS?'

'That's the one!' I said.

'The rumours were right all along! It's been

hidden behind a bookshelf all this time. Let's go!' Agatha said, just as something walloped me in the back.

'Argh! I'm under attack!' I shrieked.

'That was me walking into you! When I said "let's go", I meant *get moving.*'

I harrumphed to show I was annoyed and then bravely led the way into the ROOM OF DANGEROUS AND FORBIDDEN BOOKS, which I thought sounded a bit hazardous and should probably be brought to the attention of the school governors.

Inside the room, I scanned around again.

Old-looking books, more old-looking books, even more old-looking books, floating book, ***really*** *old-looking books . . .*

Hang on . . . REWIND!

Floating book?!

'Agatha, do you see that floating book?' I said as it jerked from side to side in mid-air.

'Och, you two . . . took yer . . . sweet time!' came a strained voice.

'Gregor? Is that you?'

'Aye! Trying . . . to . . . get . . . book . . .'

'Let go, you horrible creature!'

'Agatha!' I said, shocked. 'Don't call Gregor that. He's only trying to help.'

'Lenny, that sounded nothing like me! I didn't say that!'

Before I could ask who had said it, there was a loud ***BANG***! A bookcase wobbled, and then came two louder ***THWUMP***s.

And then the book, which I was fairly certain was the *Book of Chaos*, flew through the air, landed on the floor and slammed shut.

The **SHIVER** pulsed through the air and immediately Gregor appeared in a heap on the floor in front of the wobbling bookcase. Mr Pardon shimmered into view opposite him, his glasses on the wonk, his tie the wrong way round and his hair all ruffled. He had on a long black gown, a bit like

Dr Errno and Batman wear. Agatha materialized next to me, blinking in surprise.

'The book!' she shouted.

Which I think was a mistake because she could have just grabbed it, but instead we all leaped for it at the same time.

Unfortunately, Mr Pardon was the closest and the quickest (embarrassing), and he got to it first.

'It's *my* beautiful bookums-snookums!' he said and cackled.

While I ended up in an Agatha-gargoyle sandwich with my face WAY too close to Gregor's Creeping Crevice Moss, Mr Pardon lifted the *Book of Chaos* above his head and, fair play to him, did a really excellent evil-villain laugh.

We all shouted, 'NO!'

But he only went and turned another page anyway.

And again we all felt the **SHIVER**.

That meant one page left to Armageddon!

Dun-dun-DUNNNNNNN!!!!

CHAPTER 37
AGATHA

With the three of us in a boy/spy-detective/gargoyle ball on the floor, we really weren't in the best position to deal with what the *Book of Chaos* unleashed on us next.

I tried to untangle myself from the other two so I could grab Mr Pardon, but it was impossible.

'Lenny, stop acting all limpety and let go!' I shouted.

Lenny didn't let go. He said, 'Helf me. I can't ge' my fayce out offfff Gregor's crefish.'

'You what?'

'Ma fayce's 'tuck to Gregor'sh bumf!'

'Your face is . . . stuck to Gregor's . . . Oh WOW. That's not good!'

Gregor, who had a very strange, cross-eyed expression on his face, said, 'Och no! The book has made us as sticky as tar!'

He was right. We were all completely stuck to one another.

I glanced over at Mr Pardon, worried he might make his escape, but luckily he wasn't going anywhere either. He had one hand stuck to the book, still open and aloft in the air, and the other hand stuck to the floor.

If we could unstick ourselves before him, maybe we could snatch the book.

With great effort on my part, I managed to get to my feet and partly pull Lenny to his knees. But his face was still attached to Gregor, and Gregor was also attached to me by one knobbly hand.

I yanked hard and, with a sound like tearing Velcro, managed to pull Gregor partly off Lenny. Luckily for Lenny, it was the bum part of Gregor I managed to peel away.

As soon as Lenny's face was free, he took a

huge, gasping breath and said, 'I shall never sleep again! I have seen awful things. Unspeakable things.'

Gregor was now dangling from my arm. I tried to shake him off, but he was heavy and it was tiring, and Gregor started to complain about me treating him like a flag.

For several minutes, all of us, including Mr Pardon, struggled to free ourselves. But soon we were exhausted, frustrated and still very much stuck.

'You're going to have to close the book, or we'll be trapped like this forever!' I shouted over to Mr Pardon.

'I *am* going to close the book!' he shouted back. 'And then I'm going to open it again, one final time, and turn the very last page. Are you ready for the ending, children?'

'If we say no –' Lenny began.

'I'm doing it anyway.'

Lenny rolled his eyes and muttered, 'Don't know why you bothered to ask then.'

Mr Pardon heard and said, 'For dramatic effect, obviously.'

'And, just to clarify, you mean the *end* end, right?' Lenny asked.

'Yes, the *end* end!'

'Oooh!' exclaimed Lenny excitedly. 'Then this is the bit where you tell us why you've been doing it! The reason you want an *end* end? Did you accidentally get zapped with extra-strong gamma rays from a faulty book scanner?'

Mr Pardon stared at him blankly. 'No, I did not.'

Lenny's face fell. '*Please* tell me it's something exciting. Agatha has a theory it's just because you're sad about the library, but I don't buy it.'

Mr Pardon snarled. 'I'm sick of being taken for granted. Of being underappreciated. For years, I've kept this library in perfect order, despite all you grubby little urchins coming in and messing things up. But for what?'

I think Lenny thought that was an actual question because he said, 'To be replaced by the Minerva artificially intelligenced library owls? Chin up, Mr P – it happens to us all.'

Mr Pardon turned a radishy shade of red. 'What nonsense is that idiot talking about?'

'Hey!' I shouted. 'He's not my friend, he's an idiot!'

'WHAT?' shouted Lenny.

'No! I meant the other way round! He's not an idiot, he's my friend! My best friend! Now you say you're sorry!'

But Mr Pardon didn't apologize. Instead, he carried on with his rant.

'When I found out Minerva was going to swan in and destroy my life's work, I knew what I had to do. The time had come to call upon the power of the *Book of Chaos*. For years, I've kept it safely hidden, away from temptation. But, when Dr Errno informed me where the school fundraising money was to be spent, I heard it calling to me from the ROOM OF DANGEROUS AND FORBIDDEN BOOKS. Whispering my name. *Open me, turn my pages, unleash the chaos inside . . .*'

'He's a right wee skyrocket, this one,' Gregor whispered.

'I thought, no – there must be some other way. But then, when that Bumblestrang woman showed up, with her big silver box and false promises, it called to me for a second time. I tried to resist, but resistance, I have learned, is futile. The book, my *precious* book, must be opened! The chaos must be freed!'

'Where did you even get the book from, Mr Pardon?' Lenny asked. 'I mean, you can't pick up one of those down your local bookshop.'

'I found it in this very room when I was a

young librarian.'

'Liar!' Lenny shouted.

'I did!' Mr Pardon snapped.

'Er, since when has there ever been a *young* librarian?' Lenny said. 'And I'm not sure it's a good idea to even *have* a ROOM OF DANGEROUS AND FORBIDDEN BOOKS in a school!'

'Lenny, would you let the man speak!' I said, even though I thought he might be right on both counts this time.

'As I was saying . . . for every world of order, there exists one of chaos. And now, librarian no more, I shall rain down the terror of that chaos upon you all!'

'Gah!' Lenny pouted. 'So this *is* all about you losing your job! Is librarian even a proper job? I thought it was more of a hobby, like . . . collecting conkers.'

'What are you even talking about?' I replied. 'Librarians are *really* important. They open doors to other worlds, expand children's minds, help to educate and inspire whole generations of . . .' I trailed off, realizing I probably wasn't helping the situation. 'There are other good jobs too, though, Mr Pardon. I'm sure you have some transferable skills.'

'Possibly, but let's not forget the fact that this school believes I can be replaced! By robots! Well, I shall demonstrate to Dr Errno what happens when you fire a true Custodian of Order!'

Lenny shook his head and sighed. 'It really is all about the job. So disappointing.'

'It's over, Pardon,' I said. 'Close the book, then give it to me. We have you cornered.'

'You don't, though, do you?' sneered Mr Pardon. 'Not when I have the book and you're all stuck.'

'So what *are* you going to do?' I asked.

'I'm going to close the book now. And then I'm going to open it and turn to the very last page.'

I really thought this might be the *end* end. But Mr Pardon hesitated. For quite some time. Long enough for me to wonder if maybe he'd changed his mind.

After a while, Lenny did a big blow out of his cheeks and said, 'I'm bored. I thought the end would be more exciting.'

'I'm building up to it,' Mr Pardon snapped. 'I'm just trying to figure out how to close a book with one hand.'

'I suppose this is what you should expect when the bad guy is a librarian,' Lenny continued.

'I said I'm building up to it!' Mr Pardon snarled. 'Let me concentrate!'

He started trying to flip the book shut, but he was not making easy work of it.

'I think you've lost your moment,' I said. 'If I'm honest, things are getting a bit awkward.'

'Ugh,' Lenny sighed. 'Worst ending ever.'

'I can do this,' Mr Pardon said to himself, flapping the book about madly. 'It's just quite heavy, that's all, and I've always had terribly weak wrists. I used to have these elastic bands to strengthen

them, but I haven't kept it up recently . . .'

'Honestly, least impressive bad guy in history,' Lenny said.

Gregor's stomach let out a giant rumble. 'Och, I'm getting hungry. Do ye think we could hurry this along a wee bit?'

'Would you all stop hassling me! I'm trying my best here!' Mr Pardon shouted and then flapped some more. 'I'm going to do it. Everyone knows you have to finish a story.'

'How's this for an ending?' Lenny said. 'Mr Pardon the librarian, *despite* his weak wrists, finally managed to close the book, handed it to the brilliant young spy-detectives and left Little Strangehaven Primary peacefully to make way for the cool, laser-eyed, owl-robot librarians?'

Mr Pardon's eyes narrowed.

'Is that a *maybe* I'm hearing for handing the book over?' Lenny asked.

'Never!' screamed Mr Pardon. Then, with one final and impressive flap that finally snapped the book shut, added, 'But it's a *yes* for oblivion!'

'Oh dratballs!' I said.

CHAPTER 38

LENNY

The moment Mr Pardon shut the book and we weren't sticky any more, Agatha shouted, 'GO!' and leaped towards him.

Unfortunately, when she shouted 'GO!', I assumed she meant *GO!* as in *run away as fast as your little legs can carry you* because that made WAY more sense than what she was thinking.

For some reason, Agatha thought that launching herself *at* Mr Pardon was the best thing to do. I guess she reckoned she could get the *Book of Chaos* off him before he opened it again.

She didn't, though, what with him actually holding the book and her being five metres away.

Rubbish plan, Agatha.

The SHIVER rippled through the air before Agatha had even made her first leap or Gregor and I had scrambled to our feet.

I waited for it to subside, but something was different this time.

It didn't stop.

It was almost as if it was . . .

BUILDING . . .

GROWING . . .

AMPLIFYING . . .

Until it felt like the whole room was vibrating.

'What have you done, Pardon?' Agatha said, her voice full of trembling horror. 'That was the very last page.'

'The *end* end,' I said with a gulp.

For a second, I thought I saw a flicker of doubt in Mr Pardon's eyes. But then he threw his head back and hollered, 'Bring on the Ultimate Chaos!' Which made him sound more like a WWE wrestler than a boring old librarian.

The Ultimate Chaos didn't seem *that* ultimate to begin with, though.

It started as a gentle breeze ruffling my hair and eyelashes, which was actually quite pleasant. But soon it grew stronger.

Agatha's bunches began flapping around furiously, like a couple of helicopter blades, and I wondered if she might take off.

Books flew off the shelves, and pictures were ripped from the walls. Soon everything in the library that wasn't bolted down was whirling round our heads.

'It's like an air-whirlpool!' I said.

'More commonly known as a tornado,' Agatha replied.

She just has to be a smarty-pants, even at moments of extreme peril.

I lost my footing and was pulled by the wind towards Mr Pardon, and the open *Book of Chaos*.

'It's a wee bit blustery!' Gregor said, which was a wee bit of an understatement.

'Hold on, Lenny! The book's trying to suck you in!' Agatha shouted, grabbing hold of a massive armchair.

'Thank you for pointing that out! I wouldn't have realized!' I yelled back.

'It's just a wee squall. Dinnae panic!' Gregor said, standing remarkably still, even when one of the robot owls flew towards him and bonked him on the head. I suppose he'd had a lot of practice at withstanding gales. And birds.

But I wasn't as weatherproof, and I was being pulled across the library. If I didn't do something, I'd be sucked right into the book and lost for all eternity!

So I grabbed the closest sturdy-looking thing to me.

Which just happened to be Gregor's head.

Over the noise of the wind, Gregor shouted, 'That's it! Hold on to ma swede, laddie!'

But I couldn't. Even when I used his misshapen ears as handles. The pull was just too fierce for even *my* incredible upper-body strength.

As the book continued to drag me towards it, my feet slipped out from under me. One shoe flew off and disappeared into the book's pages with a bright **FLASH!**

I needed something more solid to anchor me. I made a lunge for a chair, but it flew up and disappeared into the book too – **FLASH!** – along with a robot owl and all the other library junk that had been circling our heads.

FLASH! FLASH! FLASH!

It looked like I would be next. Death by book was a fate too terrible to think about. It sounded so *boring*.

Agatha shouted, 'Lenny, secure yourself!'

I made one final, frantic grab for a bookcase, but my hand missed, and my heart lurched, and an icy-hotness began to eat me from the toes up.

This was it. I was being sucked in.

I closed my eyes. I was all out of brilliant ideas and excellent plans.

But luckily, before I was *gone* gone, a hand grabbed my wrist.

A hard, strong hand pulling me back and out

of the *Book of Chaos*.

'Hold on, wee clansman! I've got ye!'

I'd never been so pleased to see Gregor's horribly lovely face!

In fact, if I could have, I think I *might* have kissed it, in all the excitement of not being dead.

He was clinging to the table with his toe talons and had hold of my hand with his.

'Don't let go!' I said.

'You can count on me, laddie!'

'Close the book, Mr Pardon! I almost lost my best friend!' Agatha yelled furiously. 'You can't suck up a whole school!'

'Why not? Behold the power of my bookums-snookums!'

Mr Pardon turned and angled the book towards Agatha.

'Lenny!' she screamed as she desperately clung on to the armchair.

'Hold on, Agatha!' I shouted.

'I'm trying! But my hands are slipping!' Agatha

shrieked. 'Can't . . . hold on . . . much longer!'

'Please, Mr Pardon! Close the book!' I cried.

'Never!' he shrieked. 'It wants this. *I* want this!'

I had to do something, or Agatha was going to get sucked into the book and I'd lose her forever. But she was on the other side of the room.

I needed a plan and fast.

Come on, trusty super- brain! Come on!

'Oooh, I know!' I said.

With a wrench, I pulled myself free of Gregor's grip.

'Noooo, ye wee bampot, Lenny!'

But I was already hurtling through the air feet first, like a backwards Superman, straight towards my target – Mr Pardon.

It was risky. If I missed, I'd be sucked into the *Book of Chaos* instead, but I would rather face that than have to interview for a new assistant.

I don't really mean that. What I really mean is that I couldn't be without Agatha.

But luckily I have excellent aim as well as an excellent brain, and I **SMASHED** right into Mr Pardon's unmentionables.

Speaking from recent experience, I knew his pain.

Mr Pardon dropped to his knees and the *Book of Chaos* went flying up above his head. He let out a scream of, 'Oh, Mummy!' and, in the blink of an eye, he was sucked into the book and gone!

FLASH!

The book fell to the floor and snapped shut.

The wind died.

The chaos vanished from the room.

All was silent in the library, except for the sound of our panting.

It was over. Mr Pardon was gone. Little Strangehaven Primary was safe.

And I think I might have been a hero.

Three cheers for me!

CHAPTER 39

AGATHA

In my head, I'd really thought it would be me who saved the day, on account of all my experience of being a spy-detective.

But as it turned out, even though Lenny can't work out how to open a door, and comes up with some questionable ideas, he does know how to be heroic when it really matters.

I sat there on the library floor, thinking how close I'd come to being sucked up into the *Book of Chaos*, and wondering how I could ever put into words quite how grateful I was to Lenny. How lucky I was that he was there for me when I needed him. That he'd risked everything to save me.

I should have told him that, but instead all I

said was, 'Nice job, Lenny.'

He gave me a great big smile and said, 'Did I really do OK?'

'More than OK. You did great.'

And, before I had time to tell my arms to behave, they only went and hugged him. Again! And then I started crying. And I couldn't stop and the whole thing was a bit overwhelming and

embarrassing, and I don't know how I had suddenly become so unprofessional. But, for a moment, I didn't feel like being a spy-detective any more. I just felt like being Agatha Topps.

And all I wanted to do was see my mum and dad, and Tom and George, and Iris, Mavis and Davey, and the babies Nigel and Trevor, and Scooby and Doo.

I guess almost being sucked into the *Book of Chaos* made me appreciate all the people I loved, and who loved me, and that I was really lucky to have so many of them in my life.

I guess I had seen what *true* chaos was like.

Chaos wasn't inside me, like the book had said. Sure, my home was busy and noisy, and sometimes things weren't easy. But that didn't mean we couldn't be happy. We might not have a James Bond car or automatically restocking shelves, but we did have more love under our roof than laundry, and that's saying something.

After I'd finally stopped having emotions all

over the library in front of Gregor and Lenny, I did a really big full-body shake to pull myself together, and tried to behave more professionally. After every successful mission, there's always some tidying up to do.

'Right,' I said, in my most authoritative voice, 'we'd better work out what we're going to do with *that book.*'

Gregor scampered over and picked it up. 'You're sure ye dinnae want me to eat it?'

'Definitely. What did the warning say? *If the book ceases to be, oblivion awaits both you and me?*'

'And I think we've had enough oblivion for one day,' Lenny said very correctly.

'So what *are* we going to do wi' it?' Gregor asked.

'Oooh, I know!' Lenny shouted. 'We could strap it to a rocket and blast it into space!'

'Do you have a rocket handy?' I asked.

'Or . . . we could put it in a submarine and send it to the bottom of the ocean. No one would find it there!'

'That's very true, Lenny,' I said, because I didn't want to be rude to someone who'd just saved my life. 'But again I don't have a submarine about my person just now.'

'Or we could get a huge drill and make a hole to the centre of the Earth and –'

'Lenny,' I interrupted.

'Yup?'

'Are you doing that thing where you just blurt out the first idea that comes into your head without really thinking it through?'

'Maybe.'

'Although, actually, that hole thing is not a bad idea.'

'It isn't?' Gregor and Lenny said at the same time. Although Gregor sounded entirely unconvinced and Lenny sounded much more delighted.

'I'm not suggesting we drill down to the Earth's molten core, but we *could* bury the book somewhere no one would find it.'

'I'm liking my idea,' Lenny said. 'I am on fire today!'

'My idea really,' I muttered, 'but yeah, fine. If we're all agreed, we'll bury the book . . . in my back garden . . . when everyone's asleep.'

I took the *Book of Chaos* from Gregor.

Now that's what I call a good story.

Fancy reading me again . . .?

'Not a chance!' I said, and shoved it in my backpack.

Just as I was beginning to believe that was all the excitement we could handle for one day, Jordan Wiener burst into the room, his face bright red with fear and excitement.

'Look, Dad!' he shouted, pointing to Gregor. 'I told you there was a monster! Get it!'

Gregor immediately froze. In fact, I think we all did.

Following close behind Jordan was Cleaner Wiener. He was wearing his dirty overalls and a very puzzled expression, and carrying a giant net. He put one hand on his hip, looked Gregor up and down, then turned to face Jordan.

'Son, I don't know what's gone on today, but I've a whole school to clean up and you get me in here on a wild goose chase? That's no monster – it's a gargoyle from the roof. Although Lord knows how it ended up here. But, having said that, things are all over the place. It's like a tornado ripped through the building or something.'

'But, Dad!' Jordan continued. 'It was walking and talking. I saw it.'

Jordan hurried over to Gregor and gave him a shake. Gregor stayed perfectly still.

'I don't understand . . . It was alive. It was walking along with its horrible little feet. I saw it.'

Cleaner Wiener wasn't having any of it. 'Enough, Jordan! You need to stop with the lies!' and he stomped out of the library, muttering about freak weather patterns.

'That thing's alive. I know it is.' Jordan jabbed

his finger at me, then at Lenny. 'And I'm watching you two. I'm going to prove it. You mark my words.'

Gregor folded his arms and said, 'Good luck wi' that, laddie. I think ye'll have trouble getting anyone to believe there's a walking, talking gargoyle on the loose. And I'll have ye know ma feet are *lovely*.'

Jordan was out of that library quicker than a speeding bullet. I don't think I've ever seen someone move so fast. We could hear him screaming all the way down the corridor.

CHAPTER 40

LENNY

Cleaner Wiener hadn't been lying about having a lot of work to do – the school was in a right state. On the way to our first lesson, we had to climb over desks and tables and a whole herd of papier-mâché toucans that the Year Fives had made for their Amazon art project.

Everyone was very confused about what had happened because nobody could remember. And, even more weirdly, nobody could remember Mr Pardon.

It was as though he'd never existed.

Which also meant nobody could congratulate me on being a hero and saving the school.

In fact, the very next day, Agatha and I got

hauled into Dr Errno's office because he'd had a report about us removing a statue from the school building. He called our parents in to discuss our behaviour and what should be done about us vandalizing school property!

Agatha and me, and Mr and Mrs Topps, and babies Trevor and Nigel (because they needed looking after, not because they had anything particularly useful to add), and my mum and dad all had to attend a meeting one day after school.

I didn't expect my dad to turn up, but he did.

Dr Errno talked about how he was worried we were exhibiting some concerning behaviours and that, in his experience, it was usually a cry for attention.

Most superheroes get thanked when they save the world. Not me and Agatha. We are a *cause for concern*.

Batman never has to put up with that sort of nonsense.

Anyway.

My mum cried. I tried to tell her I wasn't about to become some hardened criminal, that in fact I was a hero, but she just cried more, until I promised her that I understood that this type of behaviour was not the way to win friends and become popular.

Dad got a bit upset too. He said he was sorry for not being around, but I told him I understood that, in our line of work, sometimes things came up that were more important.

He said, 'What are you talking about, son?'

And I winked and whispered, 'Don't worry. I won't blow your cover.'

Anyway, last week I got another tiny shampoo and I'm hopeful that one day my collection might overtake all the Pez dispensers.

Agatha's parents also promised to set aside some time each evening to talk to her about her day and how she was.

We started having play dates – I mean spy-detective training – twice a week and Agatha taught me about the difference between slinking and squidding, and how to tackle even the most difficult of doors.

Which was handy because Dr Errno kept a very close eye on us for the rest of the term. So did Jordan Wiener, who was still determined to find evidence of the walking gargoyle.

But we kept Gregor well hidden. Agatha and I shared custody of him for a bit until he decided he wanted to live by himself in the school attic, where he could eat all the old bits of masonry and not get into trouble for it. And we decided that was a fine idea because we couldn't risk him going on another midnight chimney-pot-eating spree round our neighbourhoods.

And we did as I suggested and buried the *Book of Chaos* at the bottom of Agatha's garden.

Standing over the book grave, Agatha said, 'We never did figure out what it was about us that meant we were the only two who could remember the Strangeness.'

'Oooh, I know!'

'Do you? Or are you hoping that the answer will fall out of your mouth if you start talking?'

'No, *actually*. I have three suggestions – want to hear them?'

'Fire away.'

'Number one – destiny. We were always destined to be friends because there's a deep, mystical connection between us.'

'I kind of like that –'

'Like magical unicorns.'

'Er, well, I think –'

'Shh, I haven't finished. Number two – we could feel the chaos because we both had parts of our life that were chaotic. For me, maybe I could put that down to the move to a new school, and having a dad who has to be away a lot on secret spy missions. And for you, well, there's a lot going on at your house.'

Agatha looked at me with seriously goggly eyes for several long seconds. 'That's quite an intelligent gobservation.'

She sounded quite impressed, but I was saving the best for last. 'And number three – it's all down to Bernard the Belly-Button Mole.'

'You're never going to drop that, are you?'

'I just think you rule things out too easily.'

Anyway, we decided that it didn't matter what the connection was because we'd always be connected as Little Strangehaven's BEST-EVER SPY-DETECTIVE TEAM.

As well as best friends.

Which was a good thing, because at a school like Little Strangehaven Primary there are always things which need investigating, and Tuchus and Topps are the kids to do it!

THE END . . .?

The Book
of Chaos

Sam Copeland is an author, which has come as something of a surprise to him. He is from Manchester and now lives in London with two smelly cats, three smelly children and one relatively clean-smelling wife. He is the author of the bestselling *Charlie Changes Into a Chicken*, which spawned two sequels: *Charlie Turns Into a T-Rex* and *Charlie Morphs Into a Mammoth.* His other books include *Uma and the Answer to Absolutely Everything* and *Greta and the Ghost Hunters.* Despite legal threats, he refuses to stop writing.

Follow Sam online:
www.sam-copeland.com
@stubbleagent

Jenny Pearson has been awarded six mugs, one fridge magnet, one wall plaque and numerous cards for her role as Best Teacher in the World. When she is not busy being inspirational in the classroom, she would like nothing more than to relax with her two young boys, but she can't as they view her as a human climbing frame. Her debut novel, *The Super Miraculous Journey of Freddie Yates*, was shortlisted for the Costa Children's Book Award and the Waterstones Children's Book Prize and won the Laugh Out Loud book award. Her other titles are *The Incredible Record Smashers* and *Grandpa Frank's Great Big Bucket Lis*t.

Follow Jenny online:
www.jennypearsonauthor.com
@J_C_Pearson

Katie Kear is a British illustrator based in the Cotswolds and has been creating artwork for as long as she can remember. She loves creating new worlds and characters, and hopes to spread joy and happiness with her illustrations!

As a child, her favourite memories always involved books. Whether it was reading her first picture books with her mother before bed and imagining new stories for the characters, or as an older child reading chapter books into the night, she remembers always having a love for them! This is what made her pursue her career in illustration.

Katie is a graduate of the University of Gloucestershire, with a first-class BA Honours degree in illustration. In her spare time she loves drawing, adventures in nature, chocolate, stationery, the smell of cherries and finding new inspirational artists!

Robin Boyden is an illustrator who also lives in the Cotswolds and thinks Katie is copying him. He lives with his partner and their sensitive cockapoo, Lupin, who is his muse. Robin has always been drawing – ALWAYS. He began his professional career aged six, when he created his own comic and attempted to auction it off in class. With characters such as 'Tony the tennis racket' and 'Henry the sad orange', it was a shock that the comic went unsold. He is clearly not appreciated in his own time.

He also has a first-class degree (stop copying Katie, seriously) from University College Falmouth, and a master's apparently.

When not drawing, Robin likes to grow plants and pretend to know what bird is sitting in that tree over there. Robin thinks *The Wind In The Willows* is great and wishes he could write a book about Christmas.